Thank you for buying this book

Did you know that ALL the royal... Siobhan Dowd Trust? The money will be spent on bringing the joy! the fun! the delight! of reading and stories to children who have no access to books and reading, especially children in care and other unfairly disadvantaged young people.

Siobhan personally, and energetically set up the trust shortly before her tragic death from cancer in August 2007. By the terms of Siobhan's will, all royalty income derived from her four award-winning published novels and any posthumously published work will go to the Trust:

A Swift Pure Cry (2006)
The London Eye Mystery (2007)
Bog Child (2008)
Solace of the Road (2009)

Siobhan at the last, and with all her usual clarity, decided to help the most needy readers, children deprived of books and reading. You can help them too.

Please send further donations to The Siobhan Dowd Trust
David Fickling Books, 31 Beaumont Street,
Oxford, OX1 2NP
www.**siobhan**dowd**trust**.com

THE SIOBHAN DOWD TRUST
— A Swift Pure Cry for Help —

bringi... ...ost

Also by Siobhan Dowd,
for older readers:

A Swift Pure Cry
Bog Child
Solace of the Road

www.siobhandowd.co.uk

THE LONDON EYE MYSTERY

Siobhan Dowd

David Fickling Books

OXFORD · NEW YORK

31 Beaumont Street
Oxford OX1 2NP, UK

THE LONDON EYE MYSTERY
A DAVID FICKLING BOOK 978 1 849 92044 5

Published in Great Britain by David Fickling Books,
a division of Random House Children's Books

Hardback edition published 2007
Corgi Yearling edition published 2008
This edition published 2010

7 9 10 8 6

The Random House Group Limited supports The Forest Stewardship
Council (FSC®), the leading international forest certification organisation.
Our books carrying the FSC label are printed on FSC® certified paper. FSC
is the only forest certification scheme endorsed by the leading
environmental organisations, including Greenpeace. Our paper
procurement policy can be found at
www.randomhouse.co.uk/environment

MIX
Paper from
responsible sources
FSC® C016897

Set in Goudy 12/16pt

DAVID FICKLING BOOKS
31 Beaumont Street, Oxford, OX1 2NP

www.kidsatrandomhouse.co.uk

Addresses for companies within The Random House Group Limited can be found at:
www.randomhouse.co.uk/offices.htm

THE RANDOM HOUSE GROUP Limited Reg. No. 954009

A CIP catalogue record for this book is available from the British Library.

Printed and bound by CPI Group (UK) Ltd, Croydon, CR0 4YY

For Donal

Northamptonshire LRE	
Askews & Holts	

ONE

A Giant Bicycle Wheel in the Sky

My favourite thing to do in London is to fly the Eye.

On a clear day you can see for twenty-five miles in all directions because you are in the largest observation wheel ever built. You are sealed into one of the thirty-two capsules with the strangers who were next to you in the queue, and when they close the doors, the sound of the city is cut off. You begin to rise. The capsules are made of glass and steel and are hung from the rim of the wheel. As the wheel turns, the capsules use the force of gravity to stay upright. It takes thirty minutes to go a full circle.

From the top of the ride, Kat says London looks like toy-town and the cars on the roads below look like abacus beads going left and right and stopping and starting. I think London looks like London and the cars like cars, only smaller.

The best thing to see from up there is the river Thames. You can see how it loops and curves but when you are on the ground you think it is straight.

The next best thing to look at is the spokes and metallic hawsers of the Eye itself. You are looking at the only cantilevered structure of its kind on earth. It is designed like a giant bicycle wheel in the sky, supported by a massive A-frame.

It is also interesting to watch the capsules on either side of yours. You see strangers looking out, just like you are doing. The capsule that is higher than yours becomes lower than yours and the capsule that is lower becomes higher. You have to shut your eyes because it makes a strange feeling go up your oesophagus. You are glad the movement is smooth and slow.

And then your capsule goes lower and you are sad because you do not want the ride to end. You would like to go round one more time, but it's not allowed. So you get out feeling like an astronaut coming down from space, a little lighter than you were.

We took Salim to the Eye because he'd never been up before. A stranger came up to us in the queue, offering us a free ticket. We took it and gave it to

Salim. We shouldn't have done this, but we did. He went up on his own at 11.32, 24 May, and was due to come down at 12.02 the same day. He turned and waved to Kat and me as he boarded, but you couldn't see his face, just his shadow. They sealed him in with twenty other people whom we didn't know.

Kat and I tracked Salim's capsule as it made its orbit. When it reached its highest point, we both said, 'NOW!' at the same time and Kat laughed and I joined in. That's how we knew we'd been tracking the right one. We saw the people bunch up as the capsule came back down, facing northeast towards the automatic camera for the souvenir photograph. They were just dark bits of jackets, legs, dresses and sleeves.

Then the capsule landed. The doors opened and the passengers came out in twos and threes. They walked off in different directions. Their faces were smiling. Their paths probably never crossed again.

But Salim wasn't among them.

We waited for the next capsule and the next and the one after that. He still didn't appear.

Somewhere, somehow, in the thirty minutes of riding the Eye, in his sealed capsule, he had vanished off the face of the earth. This is how having a funny brain that runs on a different operating system from other people's helped me to figure out what had happened.

TWO

News of a Hurricane

It started the day the letter from Aunt Gloria
arrived.

Aunt Gloria is my mum's sister. Mum calls her
Glo and Kat calls her Auntie Glo. Dad calls
her Hurricane Gloria because he says she leaves a
trail of devastation in her wake. I asked him what
this meant. Did it mean she was clumsy like I am?
He said it wasn't so much *things* that she upset,
which wouldn't be so bad; more people and
emotions. Does that mean she is evil? I asked. Dad
said she didn't do it on purpose, so no, she wasn't
evil, she was just a handful. I asked him what being
a handful meant, and he said it meant being larger
than life. When I tried to ask what being larger than
life meant, he put his hand on my shoulder. 'Not
now, Ted,' he said.

The morning Aunt Gloria's letter came was the
same as any other. I heard the post drop as usual on
the doormat. I was on Shreddie number three, and

the radio weather forecast was saying it was set fair but with a risk of showers in the southeast. Kat was eating toast standing up, wriggling. It wasn't that she had fleas, although that's what it looked like. She was listening to her weirdo music on headphones. Which meant she wouldn't hear the weather and wouldn't wear a raincoat or bring her umbrella to school. Which meant that she would get wet and I wouldn't and this was good.

Dad was hopping round in one sock, complaining about how the washing machine had eaten all his socks and he was late. Mum was looking through the laundry bag for a spare.

'Ted, get the post,' Mum said. She was in her nurse's uniform and even I know that when her words come out short and sharp like that, you do what she asks, even though I hate leaving my Shreddies to turn to mush.

I came back with six envelopes. Kat saw me and snatched them off me and picked out a big brown envelope and a small white one. I could see our school emblem on the white one. It is like a squashed-up X and over it is a bishop's hat, which is called a mitre. Kat tried to hide it behind the big brown envelope, but Mum saw her.

'Not so fast, Katrina,' Mum said. When Mum calls Kat Katrina, you know that trouble is coming.

Kat's lips pressed up tight. She handed over the post, all items except the brown envelope, which she held up for all to see that it was addressed to her, Katrina Spark. She opened it and a catalogue came out. It was called *Hair Flair*. She walked over to the door, head nodding.

I ate Shreddies numbers seven through seventeen.

Dad started humming the theme tune of *Laurel and Hardy*, his favourite thing to watch on TV. He'd got the other sock on and was buttering toast and his hair stood on end and Mum would have said he looked 'the spit' of Stan. 'The spit' is a way to say 'exactly like' but don't ask me why. Anyway, Stan has brown hair and Dad's hair is fair, like mine, so he doesn't look *exactly* like Stan at all.

'*Katrina!*' Mum bellowed.

The eighteenth Shreddie fell off my spoon.

'What?'

'This letter from your school . . .'

'What letter from my school?'

'This letter. The one you tried to hide.'

'What about it?'

'It says you were missing last week, without a sick note. Last Tuesday.'

'Oh. Yeah.'

'Well?'

'Well, what?'

'Where were you?'

'She was AWOL, Mum,' I suggested. Kat and Mum stared at me. 'AWOL, like in the army,' I explained. 'Absent Without Leave.'

'Get stuffed, you creep,' Kat hissed. She went out and slammed the door after her.

The radio programme switched back to the news.

'Turn that thing off, Ted,' Mum said. I fiddled with the knob, but she pulled the plug out of the socket instead. There was silence. I heard Dad munching some toast.

'She's going off the rails, Ben,' Mum said to Dad.

'Off the rails,' I repeated, thinking of train accidents. I suppose Mum was saying something about Katrina being AWOL. Maybe 'off the rails' was another way of saying 'skiving', which means not going to school when you should. But I didn't dare check, not with Mum in that mood.

'Off the rails, and nobody cares,' she said.

'I used to bunk off at her age,' Dad said. 'I'd spend the day riding buses and smoking fags in the park.' My twentieth Shreddie nearly went down the wrong way. The thought of Dad with a cigarette in hand was very strange. He never smokes now. Dad tapped Mum's shoulder and when she looked up at him, he kissed her on the middle of her forehead. It gave off a funny squeak that nearly put me off the rest of my Shreddies. 'Let's discuss it tonight, Faith. I've got to run. There's a meeting about blowing up the Barracks.'

Mum's lips went up a bit. 'OK, love. Later.'

I should explain here that Dad is not a terrorist who goes around blowing up the places where soldiers live. He is a demolition expert and the

Barracks was the local name for Barrington Heights, the tallest tower block in our south London borough. It used to be where people who are socially excluded lived. Being socially excluded is a bit like being excluded from school. Instead of a head teacher telling you you have to leave, it's more that everybody in the rest of society acts like you don't exist. And you end up with all the other people who are being ignored. And you're so angry that society is treating you like this that you take drugs and shoplift and form gangs in revenge. And the people in Barrington Heights used to do all those things. Dad said it was not that the people were bad to begin with. He said the building was sick and made them sick too, a bit like a virus. So he and the council had decided to move them to new homes and blow up the building and start again.

Dad got his jacket on. He said, 'Goodbye, Ted,' to me and went out. Then Mum sat down again and went through the rest of the post. She got to the last piece, a pale lilac envelope. I saw her holding it to her nose and sniffing it, as if it was edible. Then she smiled. Her lips went right up, but her eyes went watery. This meant she was sad and happy at the same time.

'Glory be,' she whispered. She opened it and read what was inside. I ate my last three Shreddies, numbers thirty-five through thirty-seven. She put down the lilac sheet of paper and ruffled the top of my head, a thing she does sometimes which makes my hand shake itself out.

'Hold tight, Ted,' she said. 'A hurricane's coming.'

'No, it isn't,' I said. 'We're moving into a large anticyclone.' I'm a meteorologist, or will be when I grow up. So I know. Hurricanes die out halfway across the Atlantic. They rarely hit Britain. Even the one in 1987 wasn't technically a hurricane. The weatherman called Michael Fish, who is famous for getting it wrong, actually got it right. It was only a bad storm and it had no name. A real hurricane is always given a name. Like Hannah, which gusted up to 160 miles an hour in 1957, or Hugo, which flattened half of South Carolina in the USA in 1989. Or Hurricane Katrina, a category-five storm which devastated New Orleans in 2005. (I am sure it is no coincidence that one of the most catastrophic storms of all time has the same name as my sister.)

'I don't mean it *literally*,' Mum said, whisking my empty cereal bowl away from me. 'It's Hurricane Gloria who's on her way. My sister. Remember? She's coming to visit us, along with her son, Salim.'

'The ones who live in Manchester?'

'That's right. It's been more than five years since we saw them, Ted. I just don't know where the time's gone.'

It sounded like she thought time was something that comes and goes like the weather. I shook my head. 'No, Mum,' I explained. 'Time doesn't *go* anywhere.'

'It does in this house, Ted. Down a bloody black hole.'

I blinked at her, trying to figure out if she might have a point. She laughed and said she was joking and ruffled my hair again. 'Go on, Ted. Off to school with you.'

So I went on my zigzag way across the common,

thinking about time, black holes, Einstein's Theory of Relativity and storm warnings. I imagined Hurricane Gloria building up force as it drew nearer, leaving a trail of devastation in its wake. My thoughts were so good that I nearly ended up walking into the pond on the wrong side of the common and got to school only just on time. 'Down a black hole,' I said to myself as I ran across the playground. My hand shook itself out. 'Down a bloody black hole.'

THREE

The Hurricane Approaches

That night Mum read out Aunt Gloria's letter. I tried to find it so I could quote it word for word but Mum said it had probably been thrown out because our house is too small to hoard things. I remember it went something like this:

Dear Faith (that's my mum),

I want to make up. I am sorry we argued last time I visited. Salim and I are about to move to New York City, where I have been offered a job as an art curator. Please can we come and stay with you for one or two nights in the half-term holiday on our way to the airport? I know your house is small but we can squeeze in somehow. Salim says he can sleep on the ironing board.

Kat has just told me that this is not in Aunt Gloria's style. Aunt Gloria, she says, writes with much more elaborate words. According to Kat, she lets it all hang out. I am not sure what this means. Kat wrote down what she remembered of the letter and this is her version:

Darling, dearest Faith,

I'm so sorry not to have been in touch more. Life has been horribly hectic and the years have flown by like so many swallows in the sky. I really regret how we argued last time. It has been eating away at my soul. I can hardly remember now what it was all about, but I was a total mess then, having just split up with Salim's dad and not yet having discovered Transcendental Meditation. I am much more centred now.

I have some exciting news. I've been offered a high-powered job as an art curator in New York. Isn't that fabulous? Salim and I have decided to go for it. Salim is thirteen now and very grown up. He is not happy at school here. He only has one friend, who's half Asian like him, and the other boys pick on them. So it's the Big Apple for us, a big exciting adventure in our fascinating voyage through life. Can

*we drop by your place on the way? Just for a night or
two, darling? I know your house is small, but Salim
is dead keen to meet his cousins again. He says he
can sleep on the ironing board!*

So the only thing Kat and I both remember is the
part about the ironing board.

After Mum read out the letter, Dad groaned and
put his head in his hands. Kat said Auntie Glo
sounded insane and I said that Salim must be tiny if
he could expect to sleep on an ironing board. This
made Kat, Dad and Mum laugh. My hand shook
itself out and a bad feeling went up my oesophagus.
I'd been caught out again. It was like the time I'd
asked why footballers were still being kept as slaves
when slavery had been abolished, after a newsreader
announced that a Manchester United star had been
bought by another club for twelve million pounds.

When they all stopped laughing at me, Dad said
did we have to say yes and Mum said yes, we did. Kat
asked where everyone was going to sleep. Mum said
that Aunt Gloria must have Kat's room and Kat

said no way, Mum. Mum said Kat would just have to lump it and it served her right for having skived off school, because a girl who skives isn't entitled to make a fuss about sleeping on the couch for a night or two.

Kat folded her arms and her lips went inside her teeth.

'What about Salim?' I said, eyeing where the ironing board was propped against the kitchen wall.

'He'll share with you, Ted. We can blow up the lilo.'

I looked at Kat. I knew from the way her face was that she was angry. I wasn't angry, but I felt a bad pain starting in my stomach. It was the thought of a strange boy coming into my room at night and having to hear him breathe when the lights were off and him seeing me get changed into my pyjamas and not being able to listen to the shipping forecast late at night like I do when I can't sleep.

'Uh-huh-huh,' I said, with my hand flapping.

'Too right,' said Kat. 'Uh-bloody-huh-huh.'

'You'll probably end up arguing again,' Dad said to

Mum. He sounded like a weatherman when he's predicting a really bad storm. I have looked in the thesaurus for the right word and it is 'gleeful'.

'No we won't,' said Mum. 'Because I won't let it happen. Not this time. I'll just take a deep breath every time she says something annoying and in my mind's eye I'll meditate on the shape of a teapot. And since she'll be doing the same, we'll get along fine.'

I tried meditating on a teapot in my mind's eye but all I saw was hot water spilling from the spout and coming straight at me like a scalding hot tsunami wave. Which is how the thought of Aunt Gloria coming and Salim sleeping in my room made me feel. A real hurricane would have been much better.

FOUR

The Hurricane Makes Landfall

Aunt Gloria and Salim came at 6.24 p.m. on Sunday 23 May, the start of our one-week half-term holiday. It was a fine day with some scattered showers, moving northeast. Kat and I watched as a black London cab pulled up outside our house. Aunt Gloria came out first. She was tall and thin with straight black hair, cut to her shoulders. (Kat says the style is called a bob.) She wore tight jeans and dark pink sandals. You couldn't help notice her two big toes sticking out from the gap, because they were painted with matching dark pink nail polish and were very bright. But the thing I noticed most was the cigarette holder she had in her hand. A long, slim cigarette was stuck in the end and it was lit. A trail of smoke floated up from it.

Kat said Aunt Gloria looked like a fashion editor. Kat has never met a fashion editor so I don't know how she knew this.

Salim was tall and thin with jeans on, like his

mother. He wore an ordinary backpack and wheeled Aunt Gloria's suitcase on wheels behind him. His black hair was cut short. His skin was brown. Kat says it was not just brown but caramel. She says I should say that he was very good looking. She is always thinking about whether people are good looking or not. I think people just look like who they are. I suppose I am ugly because nobody has ever said I am handsome. People are always saying how pretty Kat is so I suppose she is. To me, she just looks like Kat.

So I don't know if Salim was handsome, but he looked like his thoughts were not in the same place as his body, and I liked this about him. I think this is how I often look too.

He and Aunt Gloria walked up to our front door through our front garden, which Mum says is the size of a postage stamp. In fact, it's three metres by five and I once worked out that it could fit 22,500 stamps. Before they had a chance to ring the doorbell, Mum flung open the front door.

'Glo,' she said.

'Fai!' Aunt Gloria shrieked.

There was a muddle of arms and laughing and I wished I could go up to my room. Behind them Salim stood looking on. His eye and my eye met. Then he lifted his shoulders, gazed up at the sky and shook his head. Then he smiled straight at me, which meant that he and I could become friends.

And that felt good. I only had three other friends and they were all grown up. They were Mum, Dad and Mr Shepherd, my teacher at school. I didn't count Kat as my friend because she was rude to me most of the time and interrupted me when I spoke.

'Ted,' Mum was saying, 'say hello to your Auntie Glo.'

I looked at Aunt Gloria's left ear. 'Hello, Aunt Gloria.' I put out my hand for her to shake. She dragged me into a hug that smelled of cigarettes and perfume and made my nostrils itchy.

'Hello, Ted,' she said. 'Just call me Glo, won't you? That's what everyone calls me.' I escaped from between her arms. 'God, Faith,' she went on. 'He's the spit of our father. D'you remember? Dad in his suit and tie, even on holiday? Ted's the image of him.'

There was silence. It was true that I wore my school trousers and shirt every day even if I wasn't going to school. It's what I liked to do. Kat was always on at me to put on a T-shirt and jeans and be 'normal and chilled' but that made me want to wear my uniform even more.

Salim said, 'No, Mum. He looks a right cool dude. The formal look's all the rage again, didn't you know?'

'Hrumm,' I said.

'The look's a disguise, Mum. It hides the rebel within – right, Ted?'

I nodded. It felt good being called a rebel.

'Hey, Ted, shake hands?'

As I shook hands, we were eyeball to eyeball and I felt my head going off to one side in what Kat calls my duck-that's-forgotten-how-to-quack look. 'Welcome to London, Salim,' I said.

Kat pushed me aside. 'Hey, Salim,' she said, holding out her hand. 'That's some accent you have. Is that how *yers foolk tourk oop north?*'

'Hey, Kat,' said Salim, taking her hand. 'Is that how *yauw lot tork darn sarff?*'

Everyone laughed their heads off, which is not what literally happened but I like the idea of laughing heads becoming detached from bodies through extreme hilarity, so it is a good way to describe things. I didn't know what was funny but I laughed too. Mr Shepherd says it's a good idea to laugh when others do as it means you can fit in and become friends.

'How come you talk all south-Londony,' Salim continued, 'and Ted sounds like the BBC?'

'That's a very good question, Salim,' Mum said. 'Not even Ted's neurologist can explain it. But come through to the kitchen, everyone. Dinner's ready.'

In the kitchen Mum had extended the table to its full length of nearly two metres so that six could fit around it, but as the skinniest person, I had to squeeze in at the far end with my back to the patio door. Mum had covered the surface with a white tablecloth and had made me lay it because that was my job. Then Kat went round checking I'd put everything the right way round. This was unnecessary as I'm very good at laying tables. I think of the knife, spoon and fork as an electric current. The knife feeds the end of the spoon and the front of the spoon feeds the prongs of the fork, and the table edge is the last part. And between each object is a ninety-degree angle, so the circuit becomes a perfect square. And if you do it that way, nothing ever goes wrong.

Kat had put flowers from the garden in a glass vase in the middle and a wooden board with stacks of bread. She'd put out our best tumblers for drinks and folded up paper serviettes into them so that each one stood up over the glass rim like a mitre, our school emblem. She added wineglasses for Dad, Mum and Aunt Gloria. She'd tried putting one at her own place but Mum whisked it away and called Kat Madame Minx, which is what she calls Kat when she is annoyed with her, but only moderately.

We all sat down. Mum served out chicken casserole, one of my favourite things to eat, from a big orange pot. Aunt Gloria talked a lot. She said she and Salim were 'dead excited' to be leaving Manchester as they'd had enough of the rain. I tried to point out that the number of wet hours in the north was far less than people realized but she'd already moved on to what a 'dead fast' city New York was. I knew by then how people often say 'dead' when they mean 'very' so I didn't need to ask about that, but I did ask her how a city could be fast.

'Well, Ted,' she said. 'Everything in New York moves in quick motion. Like a film, speeded up. People, cars, even the underground trains. They have express trains that flash past the boring stops. When you're there, you feel as if time itself is rushing by at twice the normal rate.'

'Which means, Mum,' Salim said, 'you'll grow old twice as fast in Manhattan.'

Aunt Gloria laughed. She put an arm out and touched Salim's shoulder. 'He's such a joker, my boy.'

Salim's eyes stared at the tablecloth and I saw his lips move but no sound came out. Then he saw me looking at him and his eyes looked up to the ceiling and he tapped his temple and pointed at Aunt Gloria, grinning. Kat said later that this was body language for how Salim thought his mother was crazy. Next he took a mobile phone out of his pocket and put it next to his plate and looked at it very seriously.

Mum passed Aunt Gloria the bread. Aunt Gloria said she was off wheat of all kinds because of being on a gluten-free diet.

'My nutritionist swears by it,' she said.

'Aunt Gloria,' I said. I took a slice for myself. 'Wouldn't it be better for your health to give up cigarettes?' Dad coughed as if something had gone down the wrong way. 'I read some interesting figures yesterday. If everyone in Britain gave up smoking, the National Health Service would save—'

'Ted!' Mum said.

Aunt Gloria chuckled. 'No, Fai, Ted's right to ask. Trouble is, Ted, I'm totally hooked on nicotine and can take or leave bread.' She looked over to Kat. '*You* don't smoke, do you, Kat?'

Kat twisted her serviette around on itself. 'Course not.'

I frowned because I'd seen Kat with a cigarette in her mouth with her school friends only the week before. 'But Kat, that's—'

'What do *you* think about going to New York, Salim?' Kat interrupted.

Salim hunched up his shoulders and smiled but didn't look up from his mobile.

'He'll love it,' said Aunt Gloria. 'I just know. The Empire State Building. The Chrysler. Salim adores big buildings. He wants to be an architect one day. Isn't that right, love?'

'Yeah, s'pose,' Salim said. His mobile started ringing with the theme music of James Bond. He said, 'Excuse me,' and rushed away from the table and out into the hall to answer it. This time I saw Aunt Gloria's eyes go up to the ceiling.

While Salim was gone a conversation started about what we should do tomorrow. Dad had to go to work but Mum had the day off from being a nurse and it was half term so the five of us could go sightseeing, she said. Kat wanted to ride a riverboat. I wanted to visit the Science Museum. Mum wanted to go to Covent Garden to see the buskers. Aunt Gloria wanted to go to all the art museums. Salim returned, putting his mobile back in his pocket.

'Salim should decide,' Dad said. 'He's the visitor.'

'He wants to go up the Tate Modern, don't you?' Aunt Gloria suggested.

Salim doubled over with groans and writhed like he had been poisoned. I got to my feet in a panic and nearly put my elbow through the glass patio door. Everyone else laughed.

'He's such a practical joker!' Aunt Gloria said.

Salim stood up straight again, looking normal. He stroked the fine line of small dark hairs above his lip. 'Mum,' he said. 'Please. Not *another* art gallery.'

'But the Tate Modern's different. It's an old power station. With a vast chimney. And Tall with a capital T.'

'Yeah. But it's full of art.'

'Salim,' I said, 'if you're a practical joker, what's a theoretical joker?'

Salim considered. 'Someone who just thinks about playing jokes but never actually does them?'

I nodded. That made me the theoretical kind. I often think of pranks I could play on Kat, like telling her that a tsunami is scheduled to come up the Thames at twelve thirty and ruin her hairdo, but I never carry them out.

'What about the zoo?' Mum said. 'Or the aquarium?'

'They're not very tall,' I said.

'No,' agreed Salim. He scrunched up his eyebrows. 'I have it. Let's go to the London Eye.'

'The London Eye?' said Kat. 'We've been up twice, Salim. It's fantastic.'

'And it's tall,' I said. 'Taller than the Ferris wheel in Vienna. Technically speaking, it's not a Ferris wheel. It's designed more like a bicycle wheel. A giant bicycle wheel in the sky. It rotates once every thirty minutes and—'

Kat kicked my shin, which meant she wanted me to stop talking.

'Great,' Salim said. 'That's what I want to do. Like

Ted says. Fly the bicycle wheel in the sky. Please, Mum.'

'Supposing it's cloudy tomorrow?'

'It won't be, Aunt Gloria,' I said. 'We're in the middle of a large anticyclone and the weather is set fair.'

'But the queues!'

'Please, Mum,' Salim said. 'You and Auntie Fai can go and have coffee. Ted, Kat and I will line up to get the tickets. *Please*.'

'Oh, OK – only afterwards we'll take a *little* look at the Tate. All that art in a vast industrial space. I'd like to show Ted the Andy Warhols. He was an American pop artist who made pictures from adverts and famous people. Like Campbell's Tomato Soup tins and Marilyn Monroe.'

'I've heard of him,' said Kat. 'He was a weirdo.'

'He was a Cultural Icon,' said Aunt Gloria. 'I'd say he embodied the twentieth century. Some people even think he might have had' – she looked at Mum – 'you know. What Ted's got.'

There was a silence.

'Like I said,' Kat said. 'A weirdo.'

Mum's lips pressed up tight. I figured out that Kat had made her cross. But I didn't care. I know I'm a weirdo. My brain runs on a different operating system from other people's. I see things they don't and sometimes they see things I don't. As far as I'm concerned, if Andy Warhol was like me, then one day I'd be a cultural icon too. Instead of soup cans and movie stars, I'd be famous for my weather charts and formal suits and that would be good.

'It's a deal,' Salim said. 'Art gallery second. The Wheel first.'

Which was how we decided on the London Eye. Or as Salim called it, the Wheel.

FIVE

Night Talk

Salim slept on the lilo next to my bed that night.
I'd hardly ever had to share before. My hand
shook itself out. Salim shuffled into a sleeping bag
without saying much.

I wondered if I should start a conversation. But
what about? Small talk or big talk? I remembered
what Mum had said when I started at secondary
school last autumn. *When you meet new people, Ted,
keep the talk small.* I'd asked her what this meant.
Did it mean to use only words of one syllable?
She'd laughed and said no, it meant sticking to
everyday subjects. Like the weather? I'd asked.
And she sighed and said, 'OK, Ted. Like the
weather. Only not big weather. Small weather.'
Which meant I could talk about anticyclones and
minor depressions but not major storm systems or
global warming.

'Salim,' I said, 'do you do small talk?'

'Hey?' said Salim. He sat up. 'Nah. Small talk's

boring. It's what people do to pass time when they haven't got anything interesting to say.'

'So you prefer big talk?'

'Yeah, Ted. Big talk. Every time.'

'What do you think weather counts as? Big talk or small talk?'

'What, rain and snow and stuff?'

'Rain and snow. Storms. Fronts. Global warming.'

'Big talk. Definitely. Global warming's great. I saw this movie. All New York was under water.'

'London might be, one day,' I said.

'Nah,' Salim said. 'Not London. Not Manchester. Just New York.' He brought his knees up to his chin. 'My mum hates Manchester,' he said. 'She says she hates the rain.'

'I like rain,' I said, thinking about how all life depended on it.

'I like rain too,' said Salim. 'It's cool and calm.'

'Without it, we'd die of dehydration.'

'Too right.'

'But too much and you get a flood.'

'Yeah.' Salim smiled. 'A flood. Like Noah's Ark.'

'Some people,' I said, 'say the Bible flood was real. And that it could be coming again.'

Salim's head went off to the side and he looked straight at me. 'Why you so interested in the weather, Ted?'

I thought. 'It's a system. And I like systems. The weather system is hard to understand because there are so many variables. And variables are interesting. If the system goes wrong, it's a disaster. And some people think the system is starting to go wrong and that could mean the end of the human race. I want to be a meteorologist when I grow up so that I can predict things and help the human race to survive. But I will have to study very hard and find out about all the variables.'

Salim whistled. 'If a flood's coming, will you let me know, Ted? So I can build my ark on time?'

'I will,' I promised.

Salim lay down and I turned off the light. I listened to us both breathing. This was when I normally switch on my radio to listen to the shipping forecast. I keep it on the desk next to my bed within easy reach. Mum had said not to do it while I was sharing with Salim. My fingers were twitching under the duvet.

'Salim,' I said after a few minutes, 'are you asleep?'

'Nope. Not yet,' he said. 'It's hot.'

'It's a new area of high pressure,' I said. 'Moving in from the Atlantic.'

'Telling me.'

'What are you thinking about?' I said. I'd been thinking about convection currents, isobars and isotherms. I'd been imagining the shipping forecast. *Lundy Fastnet, variable three or four*. Perhaps Salim had been doing the same.

'Nothing much,' he said. 'What about you?'

'Weather still.'

We were quiet again. '*Becoming south or southeast five or six*,' I said out loud.

'Sorry?' said Salim.

'I'm pretending to read out the shipping forecast and instead of this calm we're having, a storm's brewing. Out at sea.'

'A storm,' he said. 'Yeah. That would ground planes.'

'It would take a very big storm system to do that.'

'Would it?'

'Gale-force eight or nine. A fog would be more likely to ground the planes.'

I heard him sit up again. 'Ted?'

'Yes?'

'You know this – this syndrome thing you've got?' he said.

'Hrumm,' I said, wondering who had told him.

'Hope you don't mind me asking. But what is it? What's it like?'

No one had ever asked me that before. I lay back on my pillow and thought. 'It's this thing in my brain,' I said.

'Yeah?'

'It's not that I'm sick.'

'No.'

'Or stupid.'

'I know that.'

'But I'm not normal either.'

'So? Who is?'

'It's like the brain is a computer,' I said. 'But mine works on a different operating system from other people's. And my wiring's different too.'

'Neat,' said Salim.

'It means I am very good at thinking about facts and how things work and the doctors say I am at the *high functioning end of the spectrum*.' I'd also once heard a doctor say to Mum that my developmental path was skewed. I didn't tell Salim this because I looked up 'skewed' in the dictionary and it said 'crooked', which makes it sound as if I am a criminal, which I am not.

'That sounds good,' Salim said.

'Yes. But I'm rubbish at things like football.'

'So am I,' said Salim. 'Tennis is my game.'

'My favourite sport is trampolining,' I said.

'Trampolining?'

'Yes. I used to have one. I jumped on it every day and it helped me to think. Then it broke.'

'Too bad. I love trampolines.'

'My syndrome means I am good at remembering

big things, like important facts about the weather.
But I'm always forgetting small things, like my
school gym bag. Mum says I have a brain like a sieve.
She means that things drop through the holes in my
memory.'

Salim laughed. 'Maybe I've got the syndrome too.
I forget things myself.'

'What things?'

'My mobile, sometimes. Or my homework.'

'I never forget my homework. Kat says that's why,
at school, they call me a neek.'

'A neek?'

'It's a cross between nerd and geek. They don't
like me because I only talk big. I'm trying to learn
how to talk small. But it's hard.'

'You know an awful lot,' Salim said. 'I can tell
from all these books.' He pointed at my shelves of
encyclopaedias. 'Why bother trying to be something
that you're not?'

'Mr Shepherd says if I learn how to be like other
people, even just on the outside, not inside, then I'll
make more friends.' Then I told him something I'd

never told anyone before. 'I don't like being different. I don't like being in my brain. Sometimes it's like a big empty space where I'm all on my own. And there's nothing else, just me.'

'Nothing at all?'

'Nothing,' I said. 'Not even the weather. Only my thoughts.'

'I know that place,' said Salim. 'I'm in there too. It gets real lonely in there, doesn't it?'

I heard him lie down again. He whistled through his teeth. 'Lonely as hell,' he muttered and was quiet.

I thought he'd fallen asleep, but a moment later he said, 'You got called a lot worse things than neek at my school. It was all boys, no girls, and really rough stuff.'

'Rough stuff?'

'Yeah. Fights and dares. One boy had a knife. I didn't like it. But then I got friendly with my mate Marcus and it got better. He and I, we were the top moshers in Nine K. Marcus used to be Paki-Boy, like you're a neek. But he isn't any longer. He's a mosher now.'

'A mosher?' I said. 'What is a mosher?'

'It's northern for "casual, cool dude". Last term we starred in this play called *The Tempest*. Marcus was a huge hit. He'll never be Paki-Boy again.'

'*The Tempest?*' I said. 'Is that about the weather?'

'Yeah. It's by Shakespeare and starts with this massive storm out at sea. It's right up your street.'

After that he did fall asleep. I lay back listening to him breathing in and out. I wondered how *The Tempest* could be right up Rivington Street, where we live. Then I realized 'up your street' was another funny thing people say that doesn't mean exactly that. My brain waves started whirling around the big hollow in my head, like molecules in a cumulonimbus cloud that's about to burst. I made up my own shipping forecast. *Malin Hebrides, northwest seven to severe gale nine, deepening low moving northeast, rain, becoming variable . . .*

A cool breeze came in through the window. Salim gave a sigh, as if he was working something out in a dream. I thought about what Aunt Gloria had said about Andy Warhol being a cultural icon and maybe having what I've got. Then I remembered how some people say Einstein had it too. My brain waves calmed down. And then I fell asleep.

SIX

We Go to the Eye

When I woke up, the sleeping bag on the lilo on the floor next to my bed was empty. I looked out of the window to do a weather check. The sun shone. The anticyclonic pattern of the recent days continued. Barometers would be set to dry and fair and isobars would be far apart, just as I'd predicted yesterday.

I found Salim with Kat in the bathroom. He had Dad's razor blade in his hand and was shaving off the faint hairs over his upper lip and laughing at the same time.

'But I thought it looked good, Salim,' Kat said.

Salim turned and winked at me. 'Thing is, the more you shave it, the more it grows back. It's like lawnmowing.'

This made Kat hoot with laughter. When owls hoot, it doesn't sound like humans laughing so I don't know why people say 'hoot' but they do. Nor could I see any logic in hairs or grass growing longer by being cut off. But I laughed too because I wanted to be Salim's friend. Then I ran a finger over my own upper lip. There were no hairs there and this was good. I wasn't sure about the idea of hairs growing on my face. For one thing shaving is dangerous. Dad often comes out of the bathroom with bits of blood-drenched toilet paper stuck to his skin. For another thing facial hair is a sign that we have evolved from apes. And when you remember that we evolved from apes, you have to admit how limited human intelligence is mostly.

Then we had breakfast. I had forty-three Shreddies, Kat had toast and Salim started on a bowl of cornflakes but didn't finish it. Then we left the house with Mum and Aunt Gloria walking behind us, talking up a storm. This is one of my favourite things people say. It doesn't mean they were arguing, which is what it might sound like. It means that they were talking non-stop and not paying attention to anything else around them. When storms happen, it is hard to pay attention to anything elses.

Kat and Salim and I walked in front together. I was on the side nearest the kerb, hopping across the cracks in the paving stones and around the lamp-posts, with my hands in my pockets, which is how I like to walk best when I'm with other people.

Then we passed the Barracks. Salim said how huge it was and I said it had twenty-four storeys and Kat said it would be flattened any day now by our dad.

'Never,' said Salim.

'Yeah,' said Kat.

'Why's it got to go?'

'Dad says it was full of drugs and needles and sui-cidal mums. And cockroaches.'

'Yuck.'

'Yeah. And the postman wouldn't deliver things there any more.'

Salim looked up at it. 'Some height.'

Then Kat pointed to another big tower. 'That's where our mum works, Salim. Guy's Tower.'

'No way.'

'Yep.'

The tower was silver and tall and I could see Salim was impressed with London because he looked at the tall buildings with his eyes wide open and his mouth open. Then we had to go down onto the tube. Kat and Salim sat next to each other and I sat two seats down between two strangers. I folded my arms across my chest to stop my hand flapping and shaking itself out, which is a habit Mr Shepherd says I must lose. I stared at the tube map of London. It is a topological map. A topological map is a very simplified map, not to scale, so with no relation to the real distances. The stops stand for places where you can get on or off or sometimes change trains, and these are ordered into straight lines with junctions, whereas in reality they are all higgledy-piggledy. If I'd been next to Salim, I would have talked about different kinds of map, and explained how topo*logical* maps should never be confused with topo*graphical* maps, but when I looked over to where Salim was sitting, Kat was showing him the silver nail polish on her finger-nails and asking him about his social life, which is the thing she always talks about. I tried to see if he was bored. When people are bored, Mr Shepherd says the muscles in their face don't do anything and they stare without really looking and he says I should always check to see if this is how people are looking when I talk to them. Salim was laughing and nudging Kat so I deduced that he was not bored, although I would have been.

We got out at Embankment Station so that we could walk over one of the Golden Jubilee Bridges and see the view. The sky was blue. The river was grey. The Eye was white. The capsules moved so slowly they hardly seemed to move at all.

Halfway across the Thames, Salim took an old-fashioned camera, the kind where you have to use a film, from his pocket.

'That's an interesting camera, Salim,' Kat said.

'My mum gave it to me for going to New York. I wanted a digital one, but she says this kind will make a better photographer of me in the long run.'

Then he snapped everything in sight, including one of Kat and me together, with the London Eye behind us. After he clicked, his mobile phone rang with its James Bond theme tune. He leaned over the bridge's rail and spoke into it like a spy on a double-o mission, as if he didn't want anyone to overhear.

'That phone of yours!' Aunt Gloria said when he'd finished the call and folded the mobile away. 'Who was it this time?'

'Just another friend,' Salim said. 'Calling from Manchester to say goodbye. Let's keep going. We're running late.'

'Late for what, Salim?' I asked.

'Late for the Wheel.'

'You can't be late for the London Eye,' I said. 'It turns all day long, two times an hour, every hour. Until after dark.'

Big Ben donged eleven o'clock as we reached the ticket queue, which was very long. The two mums groaned.

'It's infinite,' Mum said.

'No, it's not,' I said. 'Infinity—'

'Why don't we come back later and go to the Tate first?' Aunt Gloria said.

'You promised!' Salim shouted. He stamped his foot and his eyebrows went down over his eyes.

'Salim's right,' Mum said. 'We did promise, Glo. Let's stick to last night's plan. Here, Kat. Take this . . .' She handed Kat some money in large notes. 'You get the tickets and Gloria and I will sit at the café over there and wait. When you've got them, we'll join you in the queue.'

Kat's eyes went large and round as she took the money. She put it carefully away in her leopard-skin backpack. Then she, Salim and I found the end of the ticket queue and joined it. A lady in front asked the lady in front of her if she knew how long the wait was and the lady two people up the queue said it was half an hour to get tickets and another half-hour to board.

'A whole hour,' Kat groaned. 'Maybe that *is* too long.'

'Kat,' I said, 'an hour is a Drop in the Eternal Ocean of Time.' This is what Father Russell at our church said once about the human lifespan.

Salim grinned. 'Too right.' He took out his camera

again and did another shot from where we were standing. I asked if I could take one.

'Don't let him, Salim,' Kat said. 'Ted's useless at stuff like that. You'll end up with a paving stone and half a trainer.'

But Salim didn't listen. He gave me the camera and I aimed through the viewfinder to the crux of the wheel. It jogged when I pressed the button. I took the camera away from my eye to see a man walking towards us. He wore an old leather jacket, unzipped, and a black T-shirt with writing on it but I didn't notice what it said. He was dark-haired with an afternoon shadow on his chin, which is what Dad says he gets at weekends when he has a day off shaving. As the stranger drew near, he threw a cigarette to the ground and stubbed it out under his heel, for which he could have been fined a thousand pounds for dropping litter, but nobody seemed to notice apart from me.

He came right up. 'Excuse me,' he asked. 'Are you looking for a ticket?'

Kat explained that we were queuing for five

tickets. The strange man said he'd give us the one he had if we liked. He said he was up near the front of the queue to board but he'd changed his mind. He just couldn't face it.

'You can't face it?' said Salim. He stared at the ticket in the man's hand and then up at the Eye.

'I'm claustrophobic. I'd pass out, being stuck in one of those perspex pods.'

Forgetting that it is wrong to speak to strangers, I said, 'The pods are made of steel and glass, not perspex.'

'That's worse! Glass? No thanks.'

'The glass is reinforced. It's very strong and safe—'

'So you don't want your ticket?' Salim interrupted.

'It's yours for the taking.' The strange man held it out. 'It's the eleven-thirty boarding. That girl over there' – he turned and pointed to a girl in sunglasses and a pink fluffy jacket – 'is holding my place. They'll be boarding soon.'

Salim turned to Kat. 'What d'you say?'

'Dunno,' said Kat. 'Mum said to get tickets for everyone. It's a very nice offer but—'

My hand was shaking itself out because I had just remembered that you are not supposed to speak to strangers or accept gifts from them. But Salim had his hands up, saying, 'We'll none of us get up at the rate this queue is moving,' and Kat, I could see, was *weighing things in the balance*, which means she was deciding what to do. As the oldest, she was in charge.

'OK,' she said. 'Mum and Auntie Glo will be glad to save the money, I bet. Not to mention the time. And Ted and I've been up already. You take it, Salim. You're the guest.' The man handed over the ticket and led us over to where he'd been standing in the queue. My hand shook itself out because this meant I wouldn't be flying the Eye that day after all, and it was down to a stranger with an afternoon shadow whom we shouldn't even have talked to.

'Have fun,' the man said, smiling.

'Thanks a million,' said Salim. The edges of his lips nearly reached his ears. Kat and I kept Salim company in the queue until we got to the man who collected the tickets, who was shouting,

'Eleven-thirty boarders step this way!' Salim gave up his free ticket and winked at us and laughed. Then he went with a group of people to the zigzag ramp at the Eye's entrance.

'We'll meet you by the exit,' Kat called. 'Over there.'

Salim nodded. We saw him through the glass, advancing up the gangplank until he'd become just a shadow. He reached the spot where the pod doors opened and closed and his silhouette gave us a last wave. Then he hurried on with several others. I counted how many got on. Twenty-one, including him. The pod door closed behind them.

I looked at my watch. It said: 11.32, May 24. 'He'll be down at twelve-o-two,' I told Kat.

SEVEN

The Wheel Turns

'Let's see if we can follow Salim on his way round,' Kat said. The pod he was in was rising. By walking backwards we found we could track it as it slowly arced from six o'clock anti-clockwise to four o'clock.

While we watched, I started to tell Kat the facts I knew about the Eye: how it was not really a Ferris wheel at all and how on a clear day you can see for twenty-five miles from it, but she interrupted me and said, 'D'you like Salim, Ted?'

'He's our cousin,' I said. 'Which means we share fifty per cent of our gene pool.'

'Yeah, but d'you *like* him?'

'Hrumm. I—'

'Don't you feel anything? Ever?'

'I like him, Kat. He's my friend.'

She nodded. 'He's cute.'

'Cute,' I said. Kat calls lots of things cute, including cats, football players, movie stars and skirts and babies. Which means that cute doesn't mean much because if everything's cute, what isn't? Me, I suppose. I don't suppose Kat would ever call me cute.

'Salim's a mosher,' I said.

'A mosher?'

'It's northern for "casual, cool dude",' I said. 'And he gets lonely. He told me.'

'Really?' Kat sounded impressed. 'Perhaps it's having to move to New York. I'd be lonely if I had to leave all my friends.'

We kept watching the London Eye go round. It was like a huge clock only going anti-clockwise. Salim's pod moved from three o'clock to two o'clock just as an aeroplane flew low overhead.

'Kat?' I said.

'What?'

'What does it mean when something is up your street?'

'Huh?'

'Salim said *The Tempest* would be right up my street. He acted in it at school last term.'

Kat laughed. 'We've been reading it at school too.

Mr Moynihan keeps making me read Miranda's part and she's such a bloody dishrag.'

I considered this. 'So it's not up your street?'

'No way.' The pod was nearing one o'clock. 'What d'you think of Auntie Glo?' Kat asked.

I remembered what Dad said about her leaving a trail of devastation in her wake. Then I remembered how she'd said I was like Andy Warhol, a cultural icon. 'I don't know.'

'Me neither. I heard Dad say to Mum that Auntie Glo drives him bananas. And I found two empty bottles of wine on top of the fridge.'

In my mind's eye, Aunt Gloria turned into a motorist with driving goggles and a huge consignment of bananas in the back seat. 'You mean, she drives him bananas the same way I drive you nuts?' I said.

'Bananas. Nuts. Round the bend. Off your trolley. Whatever.'

She laughed and I joined in because it showed I knew what she meant even if I wasn't sure what was funny about Aunt Gloria making Dad feel insane.

Then Salim's pod got to its highest point, twelve o'clock, and we both said, 'NOW!' at the same time and laughed again, and this time I meant the laugh. We'd been tracking the same pod, the exact one Salim was in. My watch said 11.47. He was right on schedule and at the top the sun made the glass shine.

The pod sank slowly to nine o'clock. I remembered from the time we'd gone up before how, near the end of the ride, a souvenir photograph is taken automatically. The London Eye managers have fixed a camera into position, so that a good shot of everyone is possible against a backdrop of Big Ben. It happens somewhere between eight and seven o'clock. I saw the dark figures inside Salim's pod gather to one side, facing out northeast to where the camera was. I even made out a flash.

Then we walked back to where we'd arranged to meet Salim and waited for his pod to land. At 12.02 precisely it came back to earth. The pod doors opened. A group of six grown-up Japanese tourists came out first. Then came a fat man and woman with their two small boys who were also fat, which probably meant they all ate too much convenience food and needed to improve their diet. The girl in the fluffy jacket followed, arm in arm with her boyfriend. A big burly man in a raincoat, with white hair and a briefcase, came out next. He looked like he should have been getting off a commuter train, not the Eye. And then came a tall, thin blonde lady holding hands with a grey-haired man who was much shorter than her. Finally two African women in flowing, colourful robes came out, laughing like they'd just been at the fun fair. Four children of various ages were with them and they looked very happy.

But of Salim there was no sign.

I knew straight away that something was wrong.

'Hrumm,' I said.

Kat screwed up her face. 'I could have sworn he was in that one, with the Japanese . . .' The passengers wandered off in different directions. 'He must be on the next one.'

We waited but he wasn't. Nor the one after, or the one after that.

A bad feeling slithered up my oesophagus.

'Stay here,' Kat said, gripping my hand. 'Don't move.'

She dropped my hand and ran off. I didn't like being left on my own in those crowds. I kept blinking and looking around, thinking Salim would re-materialize. Then I started to think I'd lost Kat too. Then I realized I didn't know how to find Mum and Aunt Gloria, which meant I was lost as well. My hand flapped and I forgot about trying to stop it.

Then Kat came back. 'No sign of Salim?'

'No, Kat.'

'I bought this,' she said. 'A souvenir photo. I looked at all of them, the ones before and the ones after, but I couldn't find any with Salim in. This is the one with the Japanese and the African ladies.'

She showed me the photograph and I looked at the faces of strangers, smiling and waving at the camera. Various bits of people were chopped off, as the pod had been quite full. You could see half a face here, an arm waving there. But nothing that looked remotely like Salim.

'Salim isn't there,' I said.

Then I said, 'Salim has disappeared.'

Kat groaned. 'Mum and Auntie Glo are going to be livid.'

EIGHT

What Goes Up Doesn't Necessarily Come Down

We walked over to where Mum and Aunt Gloria were having coffee.

'Let's lie,' hissed Kat. 'About taking that ticket from a stranger.' She grabbed me by the wrist so hard it hurt.

'Lie,' I repeated. 'Hrumm. Lie.'

'We could say that Salim got lost in the crowds, that he—' She let my wrist go. 'Oh, forget it,' she said. 'I know telling a lie with you is useless. And stop doing that duck-that's-forgotten-how-to-quack look!'

We reached the table where Aunt Gloria and Mum sat talking up another storm. We stood by them in silence. A pounding started up in my ears, as if my blood pressure had shot up above normal, which is what Mum says happens to her when Kat drives her distracted.

'There you are,' Aunt Gloria said. 'Have you got the tickets?'

Kat waited for me to say something.

I waited for Kat to say something.

'Where's Salim?' asked Mum. 'Not still in the queue?'

'Hrumm,' I said. 'No.'

Mum looked as if Salim might be behind us. 'Where then?'

'We don't know!' Kat blurted. 'This man – he came up and offered us a ticket. For free. He'd bought it and then decided he couldn't face the ride.'

'He had claustrophobia,' I said.

'That's right. And the queue was terrible. So we took the ticket. And gave it to Salim. And Salim went up on his own. And he didn't come down.'

Aunt Gloria shaded her eyes and looked up. 'So he's up there somewhere,' she said, smiling.

Kat had a hand to her mouth and her fingers were wriggling like worms. I'd never seen her act like this before. 'No,' she said. 'He went up ages ago. Ted and I tracked his pod. But when it came down – he wasn't on it.'

Mum's face scrunched up, which meant she was

a) puzzled or b) cross or c) both. 'What on earth do you mean, he wasn't on it?'

'He went up, Mum,' I repeated. 'But he didn't come down.' My hand flapped and Mum's mouth went round like an O. 'He defied the law of gravity, Mum. He went up but he didn't come down. Which means Newton got it wrong. Hrumm.'

Mum looked more cross than puzzled by now. But Aunt Gloria's face remained smooth like paper without a crease. 'Bet I know what happened,' she said, smiling.

'What?' we all said.

'He probably went round one more time.'

The simplicity of this solution struck Kat and me at once.

'That's it. He just stayed on,' said Kat.

I looked at my watch. 'In which case he'll land at twelve thirty-two.'

We went back to the Eye, this time with Mum. Aunt Gloria said she would stay where she was, because Salim would know where to find her if we missed him.

We watched several pods open and close, but no Salim. 12.32 came and went. No Salim. Mum asked the staff if they could help. A woman from customer services came to talk to us. She said she'd like to help but couldn't. She said that the London Eye management policy states that children are not supposed to ride without an adult accompanying them.

Mum's eyebrows met in the middle. 'Kat,' she said, 'I relied on you. You should never have accepted that ticket. You should never have let Salim go up on his own.'

Something terrible happened then. Kat started crying. She hadn't done that in ages. She pressed her knuckles up against her cheekbones. 'It's always my fault. Never Ted's. I'm always to blame. Ted never does anything wrong.'

'You're older, Kat. But obviously not much wiser.'

Mum bit her lip and they both stared at each other.

'Why don't we call his mobile?' I said.

Mum frowned as if I'd said something stupid; then

her face cleared (which is what you say when some-one's been looking unhappy and then they suddenly cheer up, and I like this phrase because it is another weather metaphor. A face can clear just like the sky can when a dark cumulonimbus cloud has passed over and the sun comes out again). 'Of course! Ted,' Mum said, smiling, 'you're a genius. We should have thought of that right away.'

We hurried back to where Aunt Gloria was wait-ing at the table. There was no sign of Salim. When she saw us come back without him, she gave a big sigh. 'Where has that boy *got* to?' she said.

Mum picked up Aunt Gloria's handbag. 'Call him. Get your mobile out. Give him a call.'

'OK,' Aunt Gloria said. 'He's probably only a few yards away.'

She pressed some buttons and put the phone to her ear with a smile and a nod of her head. Then her expression did the opposite of 'clear'. It clouded over.

'*The mobile phone you are calling has been switched off,*' she repeated. '*Please try later.*'

She dropped the phone down on the table. Her lips trembled.

'Why's his phone off?' she whispered. 'Why?'

Kat said later that we spent the next hour darting around the South Bank like headless chickens. It is a puzzling fact that chickens can run around in a frenzy for some seconds after being decapitated, but I do not think they do this for a whole hour. We looked everywhere but there was no sign of Salim. We went back to the staff, who called in the police. A constable took our names and addresses. He asked if we thought Salim knew his way back to our house. Probably, we said. Then he told us to do three things:

a) keep trying his phone
b) go home and wait, and
c) try not to worry.

He said he would report Salim's disappearance to the rest of the squad on duty in the area. If he hadn't reappeared in a few hours, an officer would visit us.

Kat tried to explain about how Salim had vanished sometime after getting *on* the wheel and before getting *off*. He looked at her as if she was imagining it.

'Children don't evaporate into thin air,' he said. 'Not in my experience.'

So then we did b) and went home to wait. We were hoping to see Salim in our front garden but he wasn't there. So Aunt Gloria did a), that is, she pressed and repressed the redial button on her mobile phone. Mum got her inside and made tea. Kat fetched a china plate and arranged some chocolate fingers on it. This was Mum and Kat's way of trying to do c). But nobody ate any. We all tried not to worry but nobody succeeded.

Then Mum called Dad and told him what had happened. He said he was round the corner at the Barracks and nearly finished for the day. He'd come home to see if there was anything he could do to help. Mum hung up. Immediately the phone rang. Aunt Gloria grabbed it.

'Salim!' she said loudly.

She listened for a few seconds and her face turned into a mini ice age (that's my own expression and I hope you can guess what it means). She slammed the phone down.

'Some man,' she said, 'selling conservatory windows.' She made it sound as if selling conservatory windows was a crime against humanity. She looked at the clock on the mantelpiece.

'Three hours,' she said. 'He's been gone three hours. This hasn't happened before.'

Then she started pacing up and down the room, punching one fist into the palm of another. It was very interesting to watch. I wondered what kind of weather she could be compared to and decided on a thunderstorm, very localized, with forked lightning.

'Salim,' she said, as if he were in the room, 'I'll have your guts for garters.'

I had never heard this before and wondered what garters were. Kat told me later that they are what women used to wear around their thighs to keep their stockings up and they are elasticated. I do not think guts would be a tidy way of doing this.

Then Aunt Gloria said, 'Oh, my boy, what have they done to you?'

I wondered whom she meant by 'they'.

Then, 'You'd better be back by Wednesday or we'll miss our flight to New York.'

Then, 'That stupid policeman. Saying not to worry. I'll bet *he* doesn't have children.'

Then, 'Supposing some terrible gang has abducted him? Oh, mercy, mercy, no!'

Then she noticed me watching her.

'What are *you* staring at?' She pointed a pink-lacquered fingernail at me and jabbed the air. 'If you hadn't suggested going to the London Eye, this would never have happened. You and your bloody bicycle wheel in the sky!' She flopped onto the sofa and made a wailing sound. 'Oh, Ted. I'm sorry. I didn't mean that.'

'Glo!' Mum said, rushing to sit beside her. 'Calm down, love.' She flapped her hand at me as if I was an annoying fly. I figured out that this meant she didn't want me anywhere nearby.

I went to see Kat, who was in the kitchen sitting

at the table. She had her headphones on and her head down on her arms so she couldn't see me or hear me.

So I went up to my room.

NINE

Dodos, Brigantines and Lords

I jumped onto my bed, down next to the lilo where Salim had slept the night before, and banged my fist against the wall, then jumped up on the bed again and down again, wall again, and I went, '*Hrumm, hrumm,*' bed again, floor again . . . This was the routine I'd had when I was small, before Mum and Dad bought me the trampoline. Then the trampoline came and I jumped on that instead. Then the trampoline broke, but I didn't go back to the old routine because Mum said it would damage the walls and furniture now that I was bigger.

So I hadn't done the routine in years. I'd forgotten how good it felt.

When I was tired of jumping, I got out some volumes of my encyclopaedia and curled up on my bed against the wall and looked at some interesting entries.

There was a knock on the door. Kat came in.

'Ted,' she said. She closed the door behind her and

leaned against it. 'You've still got your jacket on. Why do you always forget to take it off?'

I shrugged and drew it closer around me.

'Ted, I need you now,' Kat said. She did something odd, which was she sat on the bed next to me. 'You're all I've got. Mum isn't talking to me. Auntie Glo thinks I'm Satan in disguise. Dad's home from work now, but he just shakes his head every time I open my mouth.'

I looked up. 'The dodo disappeared, Kat,' I said.

'What?'

'The dodo. It dropped off the evolutionary path.'

'Right. The dodo. So?'

'It disappeared. Darwin would say it wasn't adaptable enough to survive, so it didn't.'

'I don't think Salim's dropped off the evolutionary path, Ted.'

'No, I know. But I've been thinking about disappearances,' I said. 'And looking some of them up in my encyclopaedia.'

'Oh, yeah?'

'There was this lord called Lord Lucan. People

think he murdered the nanny who was looking after his children and then threw himself off a cliff in remorse. Perhaps he did. But his body never showed up, Kat. Perhaps he made it look that way, but really went off somewhere in disguise, under another name. One theory is that he went off to India and became a long-haired hippy.'

'I don't see what that's got to do with—'

'Then again, perhaps he was murdered himself. Perhaps he's buried under someone's patio.'

There was a long silence. 'That's not very helpful, Ted.'

'There was the *Mary Celeste* too. The *Mary Celeste* was a hundred-foot brigantine ship from New York. It turned up in the Bay of Gibraltar with nobody on board. It was as if they'd been beamed into outer space by aliens.'

'Ted, I don't think this is a time for joking.'

I slammed the book shut.

'OK,' Kat said. 'You weren't joking. I should know by now. You never joke. So what *do* you mean?'

I didn't really know what I meant. The only thing

that linked the dodo, Lord Lucan, the people on board the Mary Celeste and Salim was that they'd all disappeared. I sat looking at Kat's hunched-up shoulders. The room was silent apart from her breathing and mine. Somehow – it was a real effort but I managed it – I put out my hand and placed it where her shoulder hunched. It was bony and soft.

'Kat,' I said, 'you and I are together in this. People disappear. And things. Most of them reappear.'

Kat rested her hand on top of mine and I saw some tears fall down her cheeks. Her head went off to one side – she was the one who looked like a duck that's forgotten how to quack – and I felt a teardrop fall onto the hand on her shoulder. For a moment I didn't know if it was her hand or mine. I hate touching people. The wetness of the tear and the confusion of hands felt as if neither of us knew where Kat started and I ended.

'Ted,' she said, shaking her head, 'the Mary Celeste people never reappeared. Nor the dodo. Nor Lord Whatever.' She stopped and blinked back another tear. 'That policeman was right,' she went on. 'People don't just evaporate. Salim must be *somewhere*. If it's my fault he went missing, I have to find him. But I need your help. I need your brains, Ted. Nobody's better at thinking than you are.'

That was the first time Kat had ever paid me a compliment. I plunged both my hands into my jacket pockets and stared down at my trainers and went, '*Hrumm*.' Then I realized that in one of the pockets was an object that shouldn't have been there. I drew it out and Kat and I stared at it.

'Salim's camera!' whispered Kat.

TEN

Love–Hate

Kat grabbed the camera from me and held it in the palm of her hand. 'When you took that last photograph,' she said, 'in the queue for tickets . . . You must have put it away in your jacket pocket without thinking, Ted.'

I reached my hand over to take the camera back. She held it away from me.

'How did you feel, Salim,' she whispered, as if he was in the room, 'when you realized you'd got into the pod without your camera?'

I tried to take it again. She slapped my hand away. 'Keep away, Ted! It's my find.'

Typical Kat. One moment she's saying how brainy I am, the next she's assaulting me and telling lies. Predicting what Kat is going to do next makes predicting the weather seem easier than counting to three. Kat is not only more unpredictable than the weather, she is also more unpredictable than a) volcanic eruptions or b) lunatics or c) terrorist attacks. It is a fact that her name sounds like the first syllable of words like:

Catastrophe
Cataclysm
Catatonic

In other words, Kat is a *walking disaster story*, which is what Kat says about me when I drop things, but I think it applies more to her.

But sometimes, when you least expect it, Kat is nice. When I was small, she'd read stories to me about talking bears and magic wardrobes and take me over to the pond in the park to show me the ducklings. At school, she'll stick up for me in the playground when the rough boys pick on me.

Mum says we have a love–hate relationship. She says that when I was baby and Kat was two, she found Kat leaning into my buggy one day and kissing me all over my face. Maybe I squirmed, because the next thing Kat did was grab a hairbrush

and thump me on my head. Mum had to drag her
away to stop her from murdering me.

When we got older, Mum was always telling us to
play nicely together. Kat's idea of 'nice play' was
to line up her naked Barbie dolls with their savage
haircuts and strange biro markings and play
hospitals. She used toilet roll as bandages and cut
into them with nail scissors and squirted tomato
ketchup on them. She would tell me to help her as
the patient was dying. 'Pass me the scalpel!' she'd
order me.

'What scalpel?'

'Any scalpel.'

I looked about. 'There is no scalpel.'

'A pretend scalpel, Ted.'

'There is no pretend scalpel, Kat.'

'There is. It's right by your hand.'

'Kat. There is no scalpel by my hand. Only a toilet roll.'

'You're supposed to be the nurse!' she shouted.

I blinked. Nurses are supposed to be women and I
was a boy. I could not be a nurse.

'Try to play, Ted!' Mum said, looking on.

So I went, 'Mnee-mna, mnee-mna, mnee-mna!' and turned the lamp switch off and on, and after that I was always the ambulance. But Kat always wanted me to be the nurse and maybe that was why she went on being angry with me. Then my syndrome was diagnosed by the doctors.

'Why does he have to get all the interesting diseases?' she moaned to Mum and Dad.

I don't remember what they replied.

Right now, Miss Katastrophe was examining Salim's camera and I swallowed the hot huffy feeling I had back down my oesophagus.

'He used up eighteen shots,' she said. 'He kept clicking as we crossed over the bridge, remember?'

'He took one of you and me, Kat. And I took one at the Eye, just before the strange man came up who gave us the ticket.'

'The strange man,' Kat said, looking up. 'I wonder . . .'

I nodded. I'd been wondering about him too.

'Do you think these pictures might be a clue, Ted?'

'I don't know.' I tried to touch the camera one last time, but again Kat snatched it away.

She turned its sleek silver sides around in her hand. 'I wish it was digital like Dad's,' she said. 'Then we'd be able to see the pictures now. With this old-fashioned kind, you've to open it somehow.' She shook the camera and shrugged. 'Dunno how. You get the film out and take it to the camera shop to have it developed. It costs money and you have to wait. What a bloody palaver.'

She started fingering buttons and shaking it.

'I think we should give the camera back to Aunt Gloria,' I said. 'Because she is Salim's next of kin.'

'What's that got to do with it?' Kat said.

I was about to explain how the next of kin inherits the property of people who have died and how perhaps this also applies to the property of people who have disappeared, when the doorbell rang. Kat and I jumped up.

'Salim!' Kat said.

She dropped the camera on the bed and we ran out of the room and down the stairs. But in the hallway, just coming in through the front door, which Mum was holding open, wasn't Salim, only two grown-up people, a man and a woman. The man was in uniform, the woman wasn't, and this meant the opposite of what you might think: that the woman was in charge. This was because she was 'plain clothes'; he wasn't.

It was the police.

ELEVEN

Margins of Error

Minutes later, in the living room, the atmosphere was hot and close. Everyone was polite. Everybody was calm. But *you could have cut the atmosphere with a knife*. That's what people say when invisible feelings vibrate in the air, like ions do just before an electric storm.

Mum and Aunt Gloria were on the sofa. Aunt Gloria held a glass of brandy. Dad was standing, leaning back against the wall near the door. Kat and I stood beside him. The man, a detective sergeant, took notes, seated at the table. His boss, the woman, had taken another chair and was sitting in the middle of the room. She was thin and short with a blue skirt and jacket and a white blouse and her eyes moved quickly around the room like lightning strikes.

First she said she was Detective Inspector Pearce and was in charge of finding Salim. Then she asked questions. Who everyone in the family was, why

Aunt Gloria was visiting and why she planned to move to New York. Then she asked to see the contents of Salim's backpack. She took his things out one by one. I looked on carefully because in good detective stories what people leave behind and don't leave behind can be a clue to where they have gone. There was a spare sweater, a pair of jeans, a pair of socks, underwear, pyjamas, another sweatshirt and a tiny towel. These didn't tell me very much. Then there was a battered paperback entitled *Murder at Twelve Thousand Feet*, a guidebook to New York, brand new, with no creases, and a tiny address book. Finally there was a Swiss Army knife and a key ring with a model of the Eiffel Tower on it, but no keys.

There were no wash things, like a toothbrush, because these were still in the bathroom, I remembered, on the shelf over the basin.

Detective Inspector Pearce held up the empty key ring with her eyes scrunched up. Aunt Gloria explained that Salim had brought the key ring back from a school trip to Paris, then that she had rented out her house in Manchester and given all but her own set of keys to the tenants. At present, she said, Salim had no keys to anywhere.

There was silence.

Then the inspector looked over to where Kat and I were standing.

'You two were the last to see Salim, I understand?' she said.

Kat told her in a quiet voice, not like her normal voice, all about the strange man, the free ticket, tracking the pod and waiting for Salim to come down, and how he hadn't.

'We should never have left them to get the tickets on their own,' Mum said when Kat finished.

The inspector's hand waved through the air. What this meant I do not know. Then she turned back to Kat. 'You say you *tracked* the pod?'

Kat nodded.

'For half an hour you did nothing but stare up and watch the London Eye go round?'

'Well . . .' Kat considered. 'We walked back, so as to be able to see better. If you're too close, you can't see the pods go round properly without getting them muddled. And we chatted a bit.'

'*Without getting them muddled,*' Inspector Pearce repeated. She interlocked her hands and rested her chin on them. '*We chatted a bit.*'

'You don't have to believe us—'

'It's not a question of believing or disbelieving.'

'But we tracked it. We did. We're sure, aren't we, Ted?'

'Hrumm,' I said. 'Sure – a hundred per cent: no, Kat.' Kat's eyes and lips scrunched up. 'Sure – ninety-eight per cent, yes,' I said.

The inspector looked at me without saying anything. The corners of her lips turned up, which meant she was slightly amused. Then she tapped her nose with her interlocked fingers. 'So,' she said. 'You'd allow for a margin of error?'

'Only a small one,' I said. 'Two per cent.'

'Two per cent?'

'In every human observation,' I explained, 'there is a margin of error. This is because our senses are not foolproof. In fact, some people believe that one hundred per cent certainty is impossible to achieve.' I stopped and put my head on one side. 'As humans, we cannot even be sure that the sun will rise the next day. Our assumption that it will do so is arrived at by a process of induction. This is a process where probability based on past observation allows us to predict things like weather patterns—'

'I've had enough of this,' Aunt Gloria interrupted. 'Sunrise, sunset, up and down wheels, tracking pods. This is not a fun fair. This is about my son. My only son. He's missing. What I want to know is, what's being done about it?'

'We're doing all we can,' Inspector Pearce said. She unlocked her fingers and smoothed her skirt. 'I know you're fretting—'

'Fretting? You make it sound as if I've lost a handbag.'

'It's early days. He's only been missing a few hours. And in the vast majority of cases, young people who disappear like Salim are found within forty-eight hours.'

'Forty-eight hours! We'll miss our flight to New York.'

'Forty-eight hours, but usually sooner. But from the word go, we take the disappearance of minors very seriously. That's why I'm here.'

'He's not a minor. He's my *boy*.'

Mum put an arm around her. 'Glo . . .' she whispered.

'We're doing everything possible,' Inspector Pearce repeated.

'Such as?' Dad said quietly. Everyone turned to look at him.

The inspector sighed. 'We've begun checking the CCTV footage of the pods. No camera can see everything or everybody, but there's no sign of anything untoward happening that morning. Just the normal shots of normal tourists, enjoying the view. We've also been taking statements from other people who rode the Eye at that time. Unfortunately the numbers run to three hundred plus. And we can only check the ones who paid by credit card. We've no way of checking those who paid cash. But again, so far nobody remembers a boy matching your son's description. We've also checked hospital admissions.' Aunt Gloria eyes went round and large at the word 'hospital'. 'But nothing.'

'Perhaps he's still just – lost?' said Dad.

'That's indeed the likeliest explanation,' Inspector Pearce said.

There was a pause. Perhaps everyone was doing what I was: imagining where 'lost' was. I pictured Salim lost on London's underground system, getting on and off trains, wandering down passages, not sure if he should be on a north- or south-bound train, confused by the colours, not knowing that black stood for the Northern Line, our line. I was thinking how if I'd sat next to him on the tube earlier in the day, instead of Kat, I could have explained all about the London Underground map being topological and how you are meant to read it and then Salim would have found his way home with no problem and perhaps be here now.

'We need some more personal details,' Inspector Pearce said. She leaned towards Aunt Gloria. 'I'd like to ask you some private questions.'

Mum got up. 'Let's leave,' she said to the rest of us.

Dad opened the living-room door, leading Kat out by the elbow, but Aunt Gloria grabbed Mum by the hand. 'You stay, Faith. I need you. Please.'

Mum sat down again. She stared over at me as I waited to see if Aunt Gloria would need me too. Mum mouthed something but no sound came out. It was as if she thought I was deaf and dumb and able to lip-read. I blinked. Then she said the word out loud. 'Scoot.'

That was the second time that day Mum had told me to go away.

I shuffled out after Dad and Kat and went into the kitchen with my hand flapping. Dad closed the kitchen door behind me. The police would find out more than I would and it wasn't fair. A heavy feeling like you get when you eat more calories than you can burn off efficiently came down inside of me. Kat had her face pressed against the fridge-freezer. A tear trickled down her cheek and she was punching the side of her head with her fist. This meant she had the same feeling. It was called 'frustration, extreme'.

TWELVE

Another Fine Mess

The wall between our kitchen and the living room was not thick, and we could hear murmuring voices.

'Well, Kat,' said Dad. 'Well, Ted.' He quoted a line from his film favourites, Laurel and Hardy. '*Another fine mess.*'

Kat started crying more and didn't seem able to stop. Dad put his hand on her shoulder but this was not a good idea because it made her cry louder.

Through her sobbing noises, I tried to hear what the voices from the living room were saying. I heard odd words. 'Salim.' 'No.' 'Never.' It was always Aunt Gloria's voice. I deduced that this was because a) she was nearer the kitchen and b) she spoke more loudly than either Mum or the inspector. Then I made out a whole sentence. This was because Aunt Gloria shouted it out like a thunderclap.

'SALIM WOULD NEVER RUN AWAY FROM ME!'

I put my hands over my ears. I felt air pushing itself against my face. My mouth opened and closed. '*Hrumm*,' I said. Dad opened the door to our back garden. It was early evening outside. He motioned for Kat and me to go out with him, but Kat shook her head. So I went out with Dad on my own. We walked down the path towards the garden shed, past our line of washing, which flapped in the breeze (light, southwesterly).

'Dad?' I said.

'Yes, Ted?'

'What's the probability that Salim has run away?'

Dad gave a scrunched-up look. 'I'd hardly blame him if he had.' Then he shook his head as if he didn't mean what he'd just said. 'I don't know, Ted. I think it's more probable he's lost somewhere, trying to get back.'

'Sixty/forty?'

'Sorry?'

'Sixty per cent probability he's lost, forty that he's run away?'

'Maybe seventy/thirty. I don't know.'

'Then why hasn't he used his phone?'

'Maybe he's run out of credit.'

'Then why isn't he answering our calls?'

'Maybe he's run out of charge.'

Dad looked up at the three-quarter moon that was rising to the east of the city. 'I know. A lot of maybes.' He sighed. 'Salim and your Aunt Gloria have a strange relationship, Ted. For all that she nags him and he backchats her, I think they are close.'

'Close? Like weather gets close?'

'No. Close, like near. Close to each other. That's why I wouldn't have thought he'd run away. Not in a strange city. Not without having anywhere to go.'

I remembered Salim's joke fit, because he didn't want to go to the art gallery. I remembered him stamping his foot when Aunt Gloria had tried to suggest leaving the Eye until later. I am good at counting things and timing things and remembering things. But I find it hard to know whether people like each other or not. I have a basic five-point code to reading people's faces, which Mr Shepherd has taught me from cartoon pictures:

1: Lips up, loads of teeth showing = very amused, happy.
2: Lips up, no teeth showing = slightly amused, pleased.
3: Lips pressed together, slightly turned down = not amused, slightly cross, or else puzzled (hard to tell which).
4: Lips pressed together, eyes scrunched up at the same time = very displeased, angry.
5: Lips round like an O and eyes wide open = startled, surprised.

I thought about Salim and the way his eyes shifted around the ground a lot and how he'd looked up towards the sky when Aunt Gloria was talking. But it didn't fit into the five-point code. I didn't know what emotion it matched. I thought of him in the queue to get on the Eye, squinting upwards, looking down, turning this way and that. I thought of him shuffling in his sleeping bag, sighing in his sleep.

Recognizing the five basic emotions is one thing. Knowing how they mix together is another thing. It is like knowing about secondary colours as well as primary colours. Blue and yellow are easy paint colours to recognize. But it isn't easy to predict that if you mix them together, you get green.

'So, if they are *close*,' I said to Dad, 'that means Salim wants to be near Aunt Gloria always and wouldn't run away?'

'Not necessarily near *always*. But there again . . .' Dad ran a hand through his hair so he looked like Stan Laurel. 'We don't really know your Aunt Gloria that well. Or Salim. It's been five years since we saw them last.' The arm of a shirt-sleeve on the line flapped into Dad's face and got tangled around his neck. He laughed, which seemed a strange thing to do when you are in the middle of a crisis. He peeled the sleeve out of his way. 'Maybe they *are* close like the weather, Ted. Combustible. Who knows? All I know is, it's another fine mess.'

THIRTEEN

The Eye of the Hurricane

Kat called out to us from the kitchen that we were wanted back in the living room. When we got there, Aunt Gloria had finished her brandy and was staring at the bottom of the glass and her lips were turned down, which meant she was sad, and her eyebrows were hunched together, which meant she was also cross. Inspector Pearce rose to her feet and promised to let us know if there was any news. Then she said there was one last thing. Did Aunt Gloria have a photograph of Salim? Aunt Gloria took a credit-card holder out of her handbag.

'I've only got this,' she said. 'It's a bit old. The rest are in the photo albums. They're on their way to New York by sea freight.' She handed the picture over.

'Your son is thirteen, you say?'

Aunt Gloria nodded. 'Fourteen in July.'

'How old is he in this?'

'Eight,' said Aunt Gloria.

The inspector said the police would need something more up to date. Aunt Gloria said, 'You can get something from his father. When you contact him.'

I remembered Salim's father only barely. He was an Indian man called Rashid and he worked as a doctor. Aunt Gloria and he had divorced years ago.

'Shouldn't you call Rashid, Glo?' Mum said. 'You never know. Salim might have gone there. It's possible.'

Aunt Gloria shook her head. 'Salim would never do that. Besides, Rashid and I are not on speaking terms. Salim goes over there every other weekend, and that's it.'

Inspector Pearce examined a knuckle on her hand as if there was something wrong with it but I could see no cuts or bruises. 'And what did he think, your former husband?' she said. 'About Salim and you going to New York?'

Aunt Gloria didn't reply.

'He must have said something about it?'

'Not a lot. I said he could have Salim for two weeks at Christmas and in the summer. That seemed fine by him.'

There was another silence.

'Who knows?' Aunt Gloria added. 'Maybe he *does* have something to do with this. That's what you're driving at, isn't it?'

Inspector Pearce tucked the snapshot into her pocket and didn't answer Aunt Gloria's question. 'This, and your description, will do for now.' She stood up. 'This is my card, with my direct phone number. I'll leave it here on the mantelpiece. If Salim comes home or gets in touch, or if you have any further thoughts, call me.'

Aunt Gloria shrugged and said nothing, but Dad said we would. Then he showed her and the other policeman to the front door and they left. I watched from the window as they got into a white and blue police car and drove away. Mum asked Kat to help her prepare some sandwiches. Aunt Gloria had another brandy. Dad came back and opened a bottle of wine. That made it just like Christmas evening except it was getting late and it was still light outside and nobody was telling jokes or acting jolly.

'Do you mind if I smoke?' said Aunt Gloria.

Nobody answered. She took the silence as permission and lit up a cigarette and sat puffing in silence, even after Kat put a plate with cheese and lettuce sandwiches on her lap. She stared into space, inhaling and exhaling. Apart from her arm travelling with the cigarette holder up to her lips on average every twelve seconds, she was still. It was a strange silence. I realized that ever since Aunt Gloria had arrived in our house she'd hardly stopped talking or moving.

'Well,' said Mum, after everybody had munched what they could of their sandwiches. (Me: two. Dad: two. Mum: one. Kat: a half. Aunt Gloria: none.)

'Well,' said Dad. I almost expected him to say 'Another fine mess' again but he didn't.

'How was work today, Ben?' Mum said. It was a question she asked him every day.

'Work?' said Dad. He shrugged. 'OK. The Barracks is empty now and all locked up. The concrete crushers go in on Thursday. I've a new job on now, down Peckham way.'

'Peckham way?' said Mum. She didn't look that interested. Her eyes stared off into space.

'Peckham Rye.'

There was another long silence. Kat kept winding a strand of hair around her little finger and then unwinding it. I wanted to ask her what she was trying to achieve but she saw me looking at her and scrunched up her face, so instead I said, 'About Salim . . .'

Everyone started.

'I've some interesting theories, which might—'

'Hush, love,' Mum said. 'This isn't the time for your theories.'

A deep silence fell on the living room after that. I heard the whirr of the central heating. A kitchen tap dripped. Dad jangled some change in his pocket. I wondered what the silence was in weather terms. It was hardly the calm after the storm. Perhaps it was a

calm in the centre of a storm: the eye of the
hurricane. I imagined a whirlwind, dark and swift,
and in the middle of it a gentle oval-shaped stillness,
shaped like a bicycle wheel seen from an angle: the
London Eye. Mum shuffled her feet. The central
heating stopped whirring. Mum said it was time to
go to bed.

'It's only nine o'clock,' Kat protested. 'Anyway,
I'm here, on the couch, remember?'

'That's enough, Kat.' Mum got up and walked over
to the window and looked out. She drew the
curtains. 'This once, you can sleep in Ted's room, on
the lilo where Salim—'

She didn't finish her sentence. But we all did in
our heads. *Where Salim slept last night.* Aunt Gloria
gave a low moan and leaned over her drink as if she
felt ill. We were all thinking the same thought.
Where in this big, dark, dangerous city was Salim
going to sleep tonight?

FOURTEEN

Eight Theories

I lay on my bed that night, trying to ignore the shuffling coming from less than a metre away. I could smell shampoo and hear breathing that reminded me of a restless panther. It was Kat, on the lilo where Salim had been the night before. The city noises came through the open window. Lorries pounded down the main road. Aircraft droned overhead. I imagined a great anvil-shaped cloud forming over southeast London and hot air rising in convection currents. There was an instability in the upper atmosphere.

I often don't sleep at night. My brain is filled with all the strange facts about the world. I switch on my reading lamp and listen to the shipping forecasts on the radio on low volume. I get out my weather books. I study the charts of isobars and isotherms. I examine photographs of what the weather leaves behind: dried-up lakes, wrecked shanty towns, mud-slides, people rowing boats around the roofs of their houses. And I plan how when I grow up I will help people prepare for the disasters and save their lives and their money and advise governments on how to manage the weather.

But tonight I couldn't switch on the light because of Kat. I think the molecules in my brain went haywire, because all I could think of were dodos chasing Lord Lucan, who was sailing away in the *Mary Celeste* towards an evening sky with a giant bicycle wheel for a moon. I saw Salim waving from the deck, just as he'd waved that last time before boarding his pod. I heard Aunt Gloria's voice saying it was me that had suggested going to the London Eye, when it hadn't been. I saw Mum's hand flicking me away like a fly.

'Ted.' Kat was awake. 'Ted.'

'Hrumm. What?'

'Are you awake?'

'Yes.'

'So'm I.' She sat upright and I saw her arm reach over for the bedside light. She switched it on and we blinked at each other. 'It's no good. We've got to talk about it.' She sat with her hands clasped around her knees and her head on her kneecaps. Her strands of brown hair flopped untidily over her shoulders.

'Hrumm,' I said.

'Hrumm, yourself,' she said.

It took me a moment to realize she was imitating me.

She smiled. 'Maybe if I sound like you, I'll think like you, Ted.'

'I don't think thinking like me is any better than thinking like you,' I said.

We listened to my alarm clock ticking.

'Ted, what strikes you as the oddest thing about Salim's disappearance?'

'The fact that he disappeared from a sealed pod,' I said.

Kat nodded. 'He went up the Eye and didn't come down.'

'Definitely odd,' I said.

'And nobody else – not the police, not Mum or Dad, not Auntie Glo – seems to realize how odd. They all ignore what we keep telling them and make out how we just weren't paying attention and missed him somehow. But that's not possible, is it?'

'Possible, yes, probable, no,' I said. 'We saw two capsules empty out before his came down and several after. I timed how long he was up with my watch. There is only a small margin of error possible.'

'So what happened? Where did he get to?'

'I have eight different theories,' I said.

Kat was impressed. 'Eight different theories?'

'Eight. One of them must be correct, unless there's one or more theories I'm missing.'

'What if I write them down?' Kat grabbed a piece of paper from my desk and I dictated to her the following list. This is what Kat wrote, with her own comment after each theory saying how likely she thought it:

1. Salim hid in the pod (under the seat, maybe) and went round three or more times, getting out when we'd given up looking. (Just possible. Worth checking out.)

2. Ted's watch went wrong. Salim got out of his pod when we weren't there to meet him. (Unlikely. Just

checked Ted's watch. 23.43. His alarm clock says same. It's keeping perfect time. Ted says he checked it five times against Big Ben while we were out today.)

3. Salim got out of his pod but we missed him somehow by accident and he didn't see us either. What parents, police think. (But we think only a 2% chance. We both kept a lookout on everybody that came out and there were never many people at once. Salim would have had to miss us too, unless . . .)

4. Salim either deliberately avoided us or was suffering from amnesia (memory loss). This theory means he must either have wanted to run away or was perhaps knocked on the head and somehow forgot about us. (But we were standing there, looking at everybody as they came off, and we still don't know how we'd have missed him even if he didn't want us to see him, or forgot what we looked like. So really as unlikely as 3.)

5. Salim spontaneously combusted. (I've never heard of this, but Ted seems to think people sometimes vanish into a puff of smoke. He says it's a rare but documented phenomenon, and works like local thunderstorms. Huh. Not likely. Hardly counts.)

6. Salim emerged from the pod in disguise. (Possible, but going by the other people who got out of the pod – the Japanese tourists, women, tiny children etc. – highly improbable. The person who looked most like Salim was the boyfriend of the girl in the pink jacket. But he was plumper, with a much fuller face. Definitely not Salim. Anyway, how would he have changed clothes without anybody in the tiny pod noticing?)

7. Salim went into a time-warp. He could be stranded in another time or even a parallel universe. (Probability factor zero, as with theory 5.)

8. Salim emerged from the pod hiding beneath somebody else's clothes.

When we got to this last theory, Kat looked at me over the top of her pen. She didn't even bother writing down her comment.

'You remember how Laurel and Hardy almost get out of the Foreign Legion camp in *The Flying Deuces*,' I said. It's the film we watch with Dad every Christmas. Ollie, the fat one, is heartbroken because the girl he loves doesn't love him and he wants to forget her and a man tells him that if he joins the Foreign Legion, he will forget her. So he joins the Foreign Legion and Stan, the thin one, joins too. But the Foreign Legion is not very nice. They have to wash an endless mountain of clothes, which would take the rest of their lives to do, so they decide to escape.

'Don't you remember?' I said. 'They hide in the robes of these Arab men as they're walking towards the gates . . .'

'I remember,' Kat said. 'And that's the daftest of the lot.'

'But – you remember those African women,' I said. 'They had long flowing robes. And there was the big man in the long raincoat . . .'

'OK, OK . . .' She rolled her eyes so that I could see only the whites. She then wrote down after theory 8: (*Can Ted hide in my clothes without Mum noticing? I don't think so. But we can try.*)

Kat looked over the list. 'They're not very promising. Are you sure there aren't any better theories?

Otherwise we're just going to have to accept that the police and all are right.'

I thought hard. Then I had what people call an inspiration. An inspiration is an idea that seems to come from nowhere. In the olden days people thought inspiration came from the gods or God (depending on if you were a polytheist or a monotheist) breathing an idea into your brain. 'There *is* a ninth theory,' I said, my hand flapping.

'Not something weird, like aliens beaming Salim up to their spaceship, or him slipping between dimensions or—'

'No, not weird,' I said. 'In fact, I think it's the best theory of all.'

But before I could say what it was, the phone rang.

FIFTEEN

Infinity

By the second ring we'd dashed to the door. Kat pushed past me, elbowing me in the stomach. By the third ring we were on the landing. We heard Dad answering on the extension in his and Mum's bedroom. We didn't dare go in but we listened. But Dad's voice is soft and I could hear nothing. Then Aunt Gloria staggered out of Kat's room in a silky pale-blue nightdress. Her eyes were wide open and her hair was messy. 'Salim!' she whispered. Her teeth chattered as if she was cold although the temperature that night was not due to drop below fifteen degrees.

She flung open Mum and Dad's bedroom door just as Dad hung up.

'Salim?' she repeated.

'No,' Dad said. 'It wasn't Salim. It was the police.'

'They've found him? Please say they've found him.'

'They're not sure . . .'

Kat was holding my arm and squeezing it hard. Her mouth was round like an O. A very big O. She was staring at Dad's face and something she saw there had made her startled. So I looked at Dad too. I could see strange movements going across his lips and eyebrows. There were small globules of sweat on his forehead. It was not an expression I'd ever seen on him before.

'What do you mean they're not sure? They've either found him or they haven't,' Aunt Gloria said. Her voice had a strange wobble in it that made a pumping start in my ears.

'It's – it's like this,' Dad said. 'They've found some-one. Not far from the London Eye. Near the river. A young Asian boy.'

That's it, I thought, remembering theory number four. They've found somebody who's lost his memory and doesn't know who he is any more. He's been wandering around all day without knowing where to go.

'That must be him,' Aunt Gloria said. 'Why didn't they bring him right here?'

'They couldn't,' Dad was saying. 'Because, you see, this boy – whoever he is, he could be anyone, anyone at all – this boy . . . this boy is . . .'

I was waiting for him to say he'd lost his memory or maybe that the blow to his head had landed him in hospital so it was not safe yet to move him. I didn't expect what came next.

'He's in the morgue.'

I won't say much about what happened next. Aunt Gloria was sick on the carpet. Mum leaped out of bed. She sobbed and hugged Aunt Gloria, saying it couldn't possibly be Salim, while Dad started throwing outdoor clothes on over his pyjamas and Kat stood there, gripping me. I turned to the door and started thumping it. Dad put a hand on my arm and the next thing I knew the police had arrived and taken Dad away to look at this young Asian boy in the morgue who might or might not be Salim. Aunt Gloria was too ill to go. She lay on the sofa, covered over in a blanket, saying, 'Salim, Salim, don't let it be you on that cold slab, Salim, Salim . . .' Her teeth chattered and

Mum sat on the arm of the sofa, stroking her hair.

Then Kat did something brave. She made a pot of tea, even though her hands were shaking. That's Kat. Horrible about small problems, like missing a bus, or being ten pence short for the CD she wants, but good about the big problems, like when Mum had a big operation the year before. She made us frozen dinners and asked Dad how his day at work had been while we ate them. Then when Mum got home, she ran up and down stairs with cups of tea, flowers and magazines and Mum said she didn't know how she'd have coped without her.

The others had tea in the living room, waiting for Dad's return, and Mum had to bring the mug up to Aunt Gloria's lips to get her to drink as if she was a baby. I brought my tea back upstairs to my room. On the desk I found the list of theories and the souvenir photo that Kat had bought at the wheel. I stared at them without seeing them. *Dover Wight Portland*, I thought; *northwest six to gale eight, becoming cyclonic* . . .

Fifty-four minutes went by between when Dad

went out of the door with the police and when he came back. That's 3,240 seconds. I read somewhere that as you get older, your brain speeds up. You think time goes by faster. So perhaps I felt the 3,240 seconds the longest. But Kat said later she was sure Aunt Gloria must have found them longer than me. She said the more agony you feel, the more time slows down. And Aunt Gloria must have been in more agony than anyone else because it was her son that might or might not be lying on that cold slab.

A young Asian boy.

Salim or not Salim.

Something terrible happened during those fifty-four minutes. No amount of making up shipping forecasts could stop me from thinking about it. Death. I realized it was real. I would die one day. Kat would die. Mum would die. Dad would die. Aunt Gloria would die. Mr Shepherd at school would die. Every living thing on this planet would die. It was not a question of *if* but *when*. Of course, I'd known about death before. But during those fifty-four minutes I really knew it. That's when I realized that there are two kinds of knowledge: shallow and deep. You can know something in theory but not know it in practice. You can know part of something but not all of it. Knowledge can be like the skin on the surface of the water in a pond, or it can go all the way down to the mud. It can be the tiny tip of the iceberg or the whole hundred per cent.

I thought of the long chain of all the days of my life and wondered how far along that chain I'd already got. Was I still just starting, halfway along, or nearing the end? If it was Salim on the cold slab, did he know when he got up this morning that he'd reached the last link on the chain?

I thought about God and immortal souls and eternity. I remembered how years ago, when Father Russell in our church taught me that God had made me, I'd asked him, 'If God made me, who made God?' Father Russell had smiled and said I was a born theologian but didn't answer my question. 'Did another God make him?' I'd said. And in my mind's eye, I saw a chain of Gods, each having made the last, going back into infinity. Father Russell had sat down beside me and said, 'There is only one God, Ted. One God who has always been there. He is outside of time. He is beyond our understanding. He is always with us.'

I wondered now about this God who was beyond our understanding. I closed my eyes. I tried to imagine him. But no matter how hard I thought, all I could see were clouds of confusion in a vast and silent universe and if I'd still had my trampoline, I would have jumped extra hard and extra high.

Dad came through the front door 3,240 seconds later. I went downstairs a different Ted from the Ted that had gone up. I had stared death in the face. When I saw Dad, I knew that he too had stared death in the face. His eyes were looking far away into the same vast void.

Mum, Aunt Gloria and Kat threw themselves at him. 'No,' he kept saying, drawing the three of them into an embrace. 'Don't worry. It wasn't Salim. It was somebody else. Some other boy.' Then he looked over their heads at me and I looked back at him, and I knew we were both thinking the same thing. The someone else, the boy-who-wasn't-Salim, the young Asian who was lying on the slab. If not Salim, who?

There were shrieks, tears, laughs, there were countless *Thank Gods*, *I-knew-it-wasn't-hims*, *I-told-yous*. I didn't say anything. Dad stood still among the confusion, shaking his head.

Then he said in a quiet way, 'It was a boy. Some young boy of the street, maybe a bit older than Salim, but smaller, brown and skinny, a bit of a moustache just like Salim had when he arrived—'

'Before he shaved it off!' Kat said.

'And the same black jeans. A kind of lost innocence in his face. A boy who'd never had much in the first place, I'd say. There was dirt in his fingernails and bruises on his arm . . .'

Dad shook himself as if he was waking up from a nightmare.

'How did he die, Dad?' Kat said.

He didn't answer. 'I need a drink, Faith,' he said. 'A Scotch.'

Kat took me by the arm. 'Ted, let's go,' she

whispered. I heard Aunt Gloria crying again, quietly this time. Kat went back upstairs and I followed her. Without saying anything, Kat curled up on the lilo and I got into bed. The boy on the slab, a boy of the streets. I turned off the light and listened to Kat's breathing, which showed that she was alive. *Dirt in his fingernails, Salim or not Salim.*

The words went round in my head like a scary nursery rhyme, echoing into infinity. It was a long time before I went to sleep.

SIXTEEN

Cloud Cover

The next day I woke up early. I looked out of the window to find thick cloud covering London. Humidity had increased overnight. If I'd been the weatherman that morning, I would have said an area of low pressure was moving in from the west, with closely packed isobars and a chance of thunder.

Kat was already up. She was sitting at my desk, arranging the list of theories on one side, the souvenir photo she'd bought at the Eye and Salim's camera on the other side. 'These are theories,' she said. 'And these are clues. I've thought it out during the night, Ted. I have a plan.'

I know about Kat's plans. They always involve doing things Mum and Dad have told us not to.

I shuffled up to her side. 'A plan,' I said.

'Three plans. First, we develop this film. The photographs may reveal another clue. You never know.'

I nodded. This seemed good.

'Then we test theory number eight.'

I wasn't sure what this involved but said nothing.

'And then we take another ride on the Eye.'

I thought about this. Revisiting the place where Salim had disappeared was a good idea. In detective stories, when the sleuth revisits the scene of the crime, he nearly always finds a clue that has been overlooked by the ordinary police. But there was a problem.

'Mum will never allow it,' I said.

'If she says no, we'll sneak out.'

'That would be wrong, Kat. Besides, we haven't got the money for the tickets.'

Kat reached for her leopard-skin backpack. She took out some large notes and three one-pound coins. 'Mum and Auntie Glo gave me this money yesterday. Remember? For the five tickets. The souvenir photo was seven pounds. This is what's left.'

'Shouldn't you give it back to Mum, Kat? Stealing is bad. It says so in the Bible.'

'Shut up, Ted. She hasn't asked for it. She's forgotten.'

'Hrumm,' I went.

Kat shrugged. 'Mum thinks it's *my* fault Salim went missing. Fine. I'll give her her money back. In my own time. It's a loan. Not stealing.'

She turned to the window, threw it open and leaned outside. She put Salim's camera to her eye and clicked eighteen times. She took eighteen photographs of our back garden with the washing on the line and beyond that the shed. I did not think these would make very interesting shots. When she finished clicking, the film rewound itself. She examined the camera carefully.

'Found it!' she said.

She pressed a button on the side and the back of the camera jumped open. She shook out the roll of film.

'That's plan A,' she said. 'Now plan B.'

She put on her long dressing gown over her nightdress and stood there with the back of the gown draped over her arm.

'C'mon,' she said.

I stared.

'Don't you want to test your theory?' she said. She picked up the sheet with the eight theories and read the last one out loud, about Salim hiding in somebody else's clothes. Now it came down to it, I didn't much like the idea of getting in under Kat's dressing gown.

'Hrumm,' I said.

She took me by the elbow and dragged me downstairs. In the hallway she made me crouch down behind her, and humped the back of the dressing gown over my shoulders. She made me put my hands around her waist and practise walking up and down. Then we walked into the kitchen. It reminded me of the time Dad had played the back half of a donkey in the school pantomime. I could hear, but not see, that Mum was washing up glasses from the night before. She must have looked round.

'Hello, Kat,' she said. Her voice had a sighing sound in it. 'What on earth's Ted doing up the back of your dressing gown?'

I got out and stood up, blinking.

'Told you,' said Kat.

'Is this some kind of joke?' Mum said.

'We were checking a theory of mine, Mum,' I said. 'About how Salim might have left the pod without us noticing. It is only one of eight—'

Mum looked at me and she looked at Kat. A grimy glass was in her hand. It dropped back into the suds. She took off her rubber gloves.

'Kat,' she said, 'can you finish this?'

Her words were ordinary but her face was a Siberian permafrost.

Kat took over the washing-up without saying a word. Mum went through to the living room and sat there, very still. 'Ted,' she called, 'I want to talk to you.'

I was in trouble. I didn't know why. 'Hrumm,' I said, going through and standing before her.

'Ted,' she said. Her left hand stroked her forehead. 'You and your theories. Salim's gone missing, Ted. It's not a game.'

'Not a game,' I repeated.

'I don't think you realize how serious it is.'

'Serious,' I agreed.

'Don't keep repeating what I say!'

'Hrumm.'

'Don't grunt. I've told you about that before. Remember?'

'Sorry, sorry . . .'

'And remember to look at me properly when I'm talking to you!'

I concentrated on making my eyes move so that instead of looking at Mum's shoulder I was looking at her face. Her eyes were small and her skin was white and her lips were turned down.

'Ted.' She leaned over and touched my hand. 'Just think for a minute. What if Auntie Glo had seen you? How would she have felt?'

My hand started to shake. 'But Mum. We've got these theories. Eight of them. And—'

'Ted. No.'

My head went off to one side. I checked out the swirls on the carpet. My hand flapped harder. Mum's usually the one to understand me in this house. She's stuck up for me countless times. When I try to explain my theories about weather systems, or other remarkable phenomena of the universe, and Kat tells me to shut up, it's Mum who tells Kat not to be rude. But since Salim disappeared, it had been the other way round. Kat was listening. Mum wasn't.

I could hear Kat in the kitchen. Plates and pans clattered. I did something I'd never done before. I didn't answer Mum. I didn't even go *hrumm*. I went back into the kitchen. I picked up a glass from the draining board and smashed it to the floor.

Kat looked at me, eyes wide.

'God, what next?' Mum wailed, coming through to the kitchen after me. 'Our best crystal.'

'Sorry, Mum,' Kat said. 'It was my fault, not Ted's. It slipped.'

But Mum had seen it happen. We all looked at the glass on the floor and I *hrummed* and my hand flapped and I didn't stop it and Mum didn't tell me to stop it. She looked on in silence while Kat got out the dustpan and brush and swept up the mess. Then she sat on a chair at the kitchen table, her head in her hands, and I knew I had made her sad and I wanted to go back to my room.

Then Dad came in. He was wearing jeans and an old shirt, which meant he thought it was the weekend and he didn't have to go to work, although he did because it was Tuesday. He went up to the sink, shuffled Kat to one side, took the mug she had just washed up, turned the cold tap on, filled it and gulped it down. He finished the water, filled the mug a second time and gulped it down again. Kat nudged me and nodded her head. There were two wine bottles and a half-empty brandy bottle and a third-empty whisky bottle on the fridge. I remembered reading that alcohol, even though it is liquid, makes you thirsty. If you're marooned in a calm sea, with barrels of wine and no water, there are two things you shouldn't do: drink the wine, or drink the sea.

(Actually, there's a third thing you shouldn't drink. Maybe you can guess what.)

'So,' Mum said. 'Someone's not going to work today.' I looked around the room wondering whom she meant.

Dad knocked back another glass. 'Someone's

already rung in sick. Feel rotten, Fai, really do. Where's Gloria?'

'Still asleep.'

'Thank the Lord for small mercies.'

'Dad . . .' Kat began. 'Mum . . .' She let out the suds, took the mug from Dad, rinsed it and upended it on the draining board. 'Ted and I . . .' she said. 'We were wondering . . . We'd like to go out today.'

Mum's lips pursed and her eyes rolled. 'After what happened yesterday, not to mention Ted breaking that glass just now! It's out of the question. You're grounded. Both of you.'

'But—'

'No buts.'

Dad cleared his throat. He took Mum by the arm and led her into the living room. He closed the door behind him. I could hear them arguing in undertones. Kat leaned over and whispered, 'Dad's on our side! I know it. He'll get Mum to let us go out. You wait and see.'

Kat was right. Forty-five minutes later she and I were walking out of the house, along with Dad.

Mum said goodbye in the hallway. Her arms darted out as I passed her and she gave me a hug. The hug was very short because she knows I do not like hugs of any kind. I saw her face up close, and it was red and blotchy, which meant she had been crying and was unhappy still. 'Have a good day, all of you,' she said. Dad took his mobile phone in case of news.

As we walked towards the tube station, Dad asked, 'Where do you two want to go?'

'The Science Museum,' I said.

Kat kicked my shin, a very rude thing to do. 'Actually, I want to go to the shopping centre first, Dad,' she said.

'Not *more* CDs, Kat.'

'Oh no. I just have to nip into the chemist's.' She held out her hand and wiggled her fingernails, which were painted silver. 'For some nail-polish remover.'

'Can't wait to see the back of that stuff,' Dad said. 'It makes you look like an alien in a B-movie.'

While Kat was in the chemist's Dad and I waited outside and he told me what a B-movie was and how films like *Creature from the Black Lagoon* or

Cat-Women of the Moon, which Dad has in his collection, were made on low budgets with poor-quality props and actors and were so bad that they were funny and had a cult following. I asked Dad what a cult following was. Dad said a cult following was a fan club of something that wasn't mainstream, which means something that only a certain number of people like. I was asking Dad how many fans it took to make something move from being side-stream to mainstream when Kat reappeared brandishing a plastic bottle of blue liquid.

'Got your paint-stripper?' Dad said to her.

'Yeah. Thanks, Dad.'

'Where next?'

'Ted had an idea, didn't you?'

'Yes, Kat. The Science Museum.'

'Not that one. The idea before that one.' Her little finger went round in a circle. She winked. Kat's behaviour, from snapping eighteen pictures of the garden shed, to making me get under her dressing gown, to darting off to buy nail-polish remover, was making my brain spin.

'Remember, Ted?'

'Hrumm. Yes. The London Eye.'

Dad stopped walking. He folded his arms and looked at me, then at Kat. 'So that's what this is about,' he said. 'You two are on a trail, huh?'

Kat did a hands-raised-shoulder-shrug. Then she grabbed Dad's arm. 'Dad, it won't do any harm. You never know. If we go back at the same time as we were there yesterday, he might even show up. He might not know his way back to our house – but anybody could find the Eye again, wherever they'd got to. We – we just wanted to have another look. Get in a pod. See what it's like. See things as Salim—'

As Salim must have seen them. It was another one of those sentences that everybody finishes in their heads, not out loud. Kat's lips trembled. I once heard Mum say that Kat had Dad wrapped around her little finger. I'd no idea what Mum was talking about. I'd looked at Kat's little finger, and imagined Dad going around it, in miniature, stretched and pummelled into an odd-looking, living ring. Dad drew Kat towards him and gave her a squeeze.

'It's really hard, Kitten, I know,' he said. 'Kitten' is what Dad called Kat when she was small. He looked up at the sky. 'The Eye it is. There's a lot of cloud, which is good and bad.'

'Why bad?' said Kat.

'We won't see that far.'

'Why good?' I said.

'Because it won't be too crowded, Ted. Which means we won't have long to queue. Let's go.'

SEVENTEEN

Lightning Strikes

When we got there, it turned out as Dad said. The crowds around the London Eye were thinner than yesterday. A large tract of cumulonimbus cloud had rolled in. The area of low pressure was approaching. It was 990 millibars and falling, I estimated. Visibility was only fair.

Getting tickets didn't take long. Soon we were in the line for the ramp up to the Eye. We got to the point where we'd parted with Salim yesterday. A security man checked us over with a hand-held machine, like a giant bubble-blowing holder. Then we walked up the ramp. It was a zigzag, a back-to-front Z.

We boarded the moving pod along with a group of eight foreign teenagers and a tired-looking mum with a folded-up buggy, her baby and her two older boys. We began to rise. I counted how many we were as we moved anti-clockwise from six to five o'clock: fourteen. (I decided not to count the baby as it was unable to walk around or look at the view and because it was too small to remember the experience.) Yesterday, in Salim's pod, I'd counted twenty-one.

I drifted over to the side of the pod where nobody else was standing. I watched the other passengers. They looked out, turned, chatted in quiet voices and clicked cameras. Kat came over and stood beside me.

'I did it,' she whispered.

'Did what?' I said.

'Shush! I dropped the film in at the chemist's. By the time we get back it will be developed.'

I thought of the eighteen shots of the back garden and the eighteen other shots, our last link to Salim. 'That is good, Kat.'

Dad joined us. 'What a view,' he said. 'Look at how tiny the cars are.'

'They're like abacus beads,' Kat said, 'going left and right.' I looked down but I couldn't say I'd ever seen abacus beads like that.

Dad pointed south. 'If you had binoculars, you could make out our street, maybe even our house.'

'Typical,' Kat said. 'You come up here, just to see what stares you in the face every day.'

Dad laughed. 'I've never seen where we live from this vantage before. There's the Barracks – looking almost handsome, if you imagine it cleaned up, maybe – and there's Guy's Tower, and there's the shopping centre. You can see its red roof . . .'

'Come and see the Houses of Parliament, Dad.'

Kat pulled him over to the other side of the pod. I took Dad's place at the southeast side and looked out but without taking in what I was seeing. We got to twelve o'clock. Visibility decreased further. The Thames estuary dissolved into cloud. I thought of the *Mary Celeste*, a ghost ship with no crew, sailing over the horizon. I thought of the last dodo dying on a remote rock. I thought of Lord Lucan standing on a cliff, deciding whether or not to throw himself off. I thought of a chain of Gods, each having been created by the next, vanishing into infinity, the great vast void. I thought of the boy on the slab, the young boy with bruises and dirty fingernails, the boy who wasn't Salim.

Where are you, Salim? I wondered. Then, suddenly, it was as if I became Salim. I felt his laughing presence inside me, almost like a ghost, while I stood looking out. I tried to imagine what he'd have done, alone among strangers in his pod. Would he have chatted to somebody? Would he have stayed quietly in a corner? I divided into two, with the Ted half asking the Salim half what had happened. But the ghost of Salim, like the dodos, lords and crew of the *Mary Celeste*, vanished before we reached nine o'clock.

An announcement came on from a speaker in the corner of the pod, suggesting that we all group together facing northeastwards towards the spiral staircase to pose for the souvenir photo.

'Shall we?' said Dad.

'Yes, let's,' said Kat.

Kat and Dad gathered on one side of the pod with the other passengers, while I stayed out at the edge, half posing, half looking at the others posing.

The camera flashed. The pod came down.

A young man with a London Eye T-shirt, a

member of staff, stood at the door beckoning us to come out. The others filed out first. Dad and I were next. But Kat hung back, her eyes darting around. She crouched down by the seats, but the man came in and shooed her out, then picked up a piece of litter that the woman holding the baby had dropped and got out himself.

'What was that all about?' Dad said.

I nearly said, 'Theory number one, being disproved,' but remembered how Mum had reacted to theory number eight.

'I thought I'd dropped something,' Kat said.

'Well, shake a leg,' Dad said. ('Shake a leg' is Dad's favourite way of saying 'Hurry up', although if you tried to run and shake a leg at the same time, you would fall over.)

Kat nudged me. We'd both realized the same thing at the same time. You couldn't stay on for another go. Exit, enter, exit, enter – it was a smooth operation.

The way out led past the souvenir photo booth, close to where we'd said we'd meet Salim. There were several television-like screens with different shots of each passenger load. Our one was number 2,903. There was Dad, there was Kat, there was the mum and her two boys and her baby. The teenage tourists were bunched around them, grinning and waving. You could only see my shoulder and ear, sticking out on the right, behind everybody else.

'Ted's cut off, and I look a fright,' Dad said. 'But you look all right, Kat.'

Kat had her arms folded and her hair was tied in what girls call a topknot. Her skinny, bony face jutted out. With her tilted chin and dark eyebrows she seemed sharper, somehow, as if she was more in focus than other people round her, or more real. You couldn't help noticing her, whether you were look-ing for her or not.

Maybe that's what being pretty meant, I thought.

'God,' she said. 'My hair looks icky.'

Dad bought the shot anyway.

Then we left the Eye and walked along the river. The Thames was flat and brown. The pleasure boats cruised along with hardly any passengers. You could hear aircraft, but not see them. The blanket of cloud grew thicker. I kept looking out for Salim. Whenever we passed a boy of about his build, with dark hair, I'd stare. But when we drew close, it was never him. Dad stopped to look out across the water. He pointed out two cormorants that dipped and dived into the water, disappearing for ages, then reappearing ten metres or more from where they'd gone down.

'Is Salim like the cormorants, Dad?'

'Sorry, Ted?'

'Will he reappear eventually? Like they do? Maybe not where he disappeared but somewhere else?'

Dad didn't answer straight away. He looked downstream, with his lips turned down, which meant he was sad. Perhaps he was thinking of the boy on the slab, the boy who might have been Salim, but wasn't. 'I certainly hope Salim is like the cormorants, Ted.'

We crossed the river to the Embankment Gardens and had sandwiches in the Park Café. When we'd finished, we walked around the beds of colourful flowers. Then, just as I'd predicted that morning, a thunderstorm started. First rain dripped, then splattered. There was a thunderclap. The instability in the upper atmosphere erupted. I thought of theory number five: spontaneous combustion. If thunder was possible, why not that?

'Good thing we're not on the Eye now,' Dad said. Lightning flashed. Ten seconds later it thundered again.

'Dad,' I said, 'the storm is three kilometres away. Even if it was nearer, your chance of being struck is approximately one in three million.'

We dashed for the underground station. By now it was raining cats and dogs (which is the strangest expression of all, but my personal favourite. When I imagine cats and dogs coming from the sky, I see white fluffy kittens and Dalmatian puppies). Then it turned to hail. The lightning and thunder were four seconds apart.

'Twelve hundred metres,' I said, 'and it is sheet lightning, which means—'

'Shut up, Ted,' Kat said. She had her jacket collar up over her head. 'I'm soaked.'

Dad looked at his watch. 'Three o'clock. No calls on the mobile. So no news.'

'Let's go home,' Kat said. 'It's too wet to stay out.'

'OK, Kat. We'll call it a day.'

We went down into the underground. By the time we were back up on street level the storm had moved away. The rain had stopped. The pavements ran with moisture.

'It was a very localized storm system,' I said.

'Dad,' said Kat, 'd'you mind if we stop by the shopping centre again? I want to get a present for Auntie Glo. Some bath oil to help her relax.'

Dad's lips went right up. 'That's a great idea, Kitten.'

We waited as Kat went into the chemist's again. She emerged with a plastic bottle of syrupy, raspberry-coloured liquid. Dad unscrewed the lid, smelled it and crinkled up his nose. This meant that he didn't think it smelled pleasant, but what he said was, 'That should do nicely.'

What he didn't see, but I did, was the top of a wallet of newly processed photos, bulging from the pocket of Kat's fur-collared jacket.

EIGHTEEN

The Ninth Theory

When we got home, there was a smog in the living room caused by Aunt Gloria's cigarettes. A smog is technically a mixture of smoke, fog and chemical fumes but this was a mixture of smoke, smoke and more smoke. Mum said there had been no news but we already knew this because Dad's mobile phone had not rung. I tried to tell her and Aunt Gloria about our trip to the London Eye but Kat started coughing and Dad said we had had a very pleasant walk by the river. Then Kat gave Aunt Gloria the bath oil, saying it was a present from both her and me, and when Aunt Gloria looked at the label, her lips went up. She said thank you, Kat, and thank you, Ted, and added that it was the kind she'd used when Salim was little.

'The little devil that he was,' she said. 'Forever pinching it. He liked the bubbles. Blowing them up. Giggling when they burst.'

Then she started crying and Mum told Kat and me to go upstairs.

Upstairs, Kat got out the wallet of photos and flicked through them at the rate of one a second. I was very excited to see them but she wouldn't let me. In eighteen seconds eighteen pictures of our back garden and the washing and the shed were all over my duvet cover. When she got to the first eighteen shots, the ones taken the morning of Salim's disappearance, she slowed down. I tried to look over her shoulder but she jerked away. She went through them twice, then dropped them on the bed as if she was no longer interested. I picked them up and looked.

'Just a set of stupid touristy shots,' Kat said. 'Like any others.'

There were scenes of the Houses of Parliament, Lambeth Bridge and the Eye, from different angles. The best shot was the one Salim had taken of Kat and me on the Jubilee footbridge. It had Kat's face and mine close together and behind us was half of the Eye and some bridge and river and sky. Kat was smiling. My head was off to one side and my eyes were looking upwards as if I was thinking. Kat was taller than me. My head ended where her chin began.

The last shot was the one I had taken. It had gone wrong. Instead of the London Eye, I had snapped some legs and headless bodies of the people near where we'd been queuing. I arranged the photos on my desk alongside the souvenir shot of the capsule in which we thought Salim had been a passenger and the list of theories.

We sat in silence.

Kat breathed out long and hard. 'I don't even know what I expected to find,' she said, shuffling the pictures about. 'I wish we'd just given Auntie Glo Salim's camera when we first found it. Now we'll have to explain why we *didn't* give it to her. And I bet when she sees Salim's last photos she'll just start crying again.' She picked up the shot of her and me on the footbridge and threw it down again. 'A clue? As if!'

I picked up the photo. 'Let's keep the photos and

the camera safe in my room until Salim returns,' I suggested.

'*If* he returns,' Kat said, biting her lip. She shook her head and swept all the photos up into a rough pile. 'But I agree. There's no point upsetting Auntie Glo. You don't have to lie, Ted. Just say nothing.' Then Kat picked up the list of theories. 'As for this' – she scrunched it up and threw it in the waste-paper basket – 'it's beyond us, Ted.'

I watched the paper crackle softly as if it was trying to re-open itself. When the corners re-appeared, I took it back out of the rubbish and smoothed it flat on the desk.

'Forget it, Ted,' Kat said.

I picked up a pen. 'Let's try a process of elimination,' I said. The world's most famous fictional detective, Sherlock Holmes, said that once you have eliminated all the possibilities, whatever remains, however improbable, must be true. I was eager to see if we could eliminate all the theories except my favourite theory of all, which was that Salim had spontaneously combusted. This would not have

SIOBHAN DOWD

been a good outcome for Aunt Gloria or for Salim, but it would mean that spontaneous combustion was a real phenomenon and my discovering this would have been an advance in science.

'Theories one and eight can go,' I began. 'Today we have proved that Salim couldn't have stayed in his capsule after it came down and he couldn't have come out hiding under somebody's else's clothes.' I crossed them out.

'Drop it, Ted.'

'That leaves six.'

'While you're at it you can cross off the one about spontaneous explosion or whatever it's called.'

'Theory number five?'

'Yeah. And the time-warp one.'

'Number seven?' My pencil hovered over the list. 'But supposing we eliminate all the others and—'

'Oh, grow up, Ted.'

I wished Kat could spontaneously combust there and then. But she didn't. Her eyebrows came close together and her lips were right down and then a tear came rolling out of her left eye and down her

144

nose. I thought of something I hadn't thought of before. Very slowly I drew a wavy line through theories five and seven even though a strange feeling went up my oesophagus.

'Done,' I said.

Kat picked up the list as if she was interested again. She brushed off the tear. 'That leaves four theories,' she said. 'Two, three, four and six.'

'And nine,' I said, remembering.

'Nine?'

'The ninth theory is the one I was going to tell you about last night,' I reminded her. 'When the phone rang. You never wrote it down.'

She took the pen from me. 'You never told me what it was. Out with it, Ted. It had better be good.'

'It is.' I started dictating. 'The ninth theory is that Salim never got on the Eye in the first place.'

Kat got halfway through writing the words, then stopped and said it was daft and I said it wasn't and she said hadn't we seen him get on and I said we had seen what we *thought* was Salim but it was just a shadow and could have been anyone.

'He turned and waved,' Kat said.

'Lots of people might have done that,' I said. 'Not just Salim.'

'But what happened to Salim, then, between when we said goodbye and when he got to the top of the ramp?'

I had not considered this. 'He might have stopped to do up his trainers and decided not to get on after all and come back down the ramp after we moved away. And then he might have looked for us but we'd vanished into the crowds. And then he might have got lost or run away or got kidnapped.'

Kat closed her eyes. 'OK, Ted. I'm reliving the moment.'

I shut my eyes too. But all I could see was the wrong-way-round Z and a line of boys, all Salim look-alikes, smiling and waving and saying goodbye and walking to the edge of a precipice.

'Ted,' Kat said. I opened my eyes. 'I have to admit it's a clever theory.'

A good tingling feeling went from my oesophagus up to my scalp. I smiled.

'But it's wrong, Ted.'

I stopped smiling. 'Wrong.'

'I don't expect you to understand. The boy who waved from the top of the ramp. The way he stood and looked back. The way he turned and walked on. It was Salim. I just know.'

'You just know?'

'It's a body-language thing.'

The good feeling I had turned bad. 'Body language' is a form of communication, like speaking English or French or Chinese, but it has no words, only gestures. Humans and chimpanzees and meerkats and stingrays can read body language by instinct without having to learn it. But according to the doctors who diagnosed me, people with my kind of syndrome can't. We have to learn it like a foreign language and this takes time.

'You mean, you saw something about the boy who waved that I didn't?'

'Yes, Ted.' Kat's voice was soft. She put a hand on my shoulder, which made the hairs on my neck stick up. 'Trust me. It was Salim we saw. It just was.'

I took the pencil back from Kat and crossed off what she'd written for theory nine. I crossed it out three times over. I'd thought it the best theory of all until then. Now it was dead, almost at birth. Dead as a dodo, you could say.

NINETEEN

The Boy on the Train

Mum came in and Kat sat on the desk, on top of the photos and the theory list.

'Hi, guys,' Mum said.

'Hi, Mum,' said Kat. She swung her legs backwards and forwards and stared into space.

'This isn't much of a half term for you, is it?'

'Don't worry, Mum. We're fine.'

Mum smiled. Then she said the police were visiting us again and we should go downstairs, in case they wanted to ask us anything. Then she went out and Kat got off the desk. She hid the theory list and the photographs in the little drawer under my desk. Then she picked up the souvenir picture and said that she'd hand it over to the police, just in case it was of some use. Then she went out of my room. I reopened the drawer. I found my favourite photo – the one Salim had taken of Kat and me on the footbridge. It looked as if a corner of the London Eye was emerging from my shoulder. Then I put it in my book of weather systems, between cyclones and anti-cyclones, where it would be safe. Then I followed Kat downstairs.

Soon the police car drew up and Mum and Aunt Gloria took the same places on the sofa and Dad showed in Detective Inspector Pearce, who was on her own. She sat on the same chair as yesterday.

Nobody said anything for a minute. Then Kat went up to her and offered her the souvenir photograph.

'I'm sorry we didn't give it to you sooner,' Kat said. 'I meant to yesterday, but we forgot, didn't we, Ted?'

'Hrumm,' I said.

Detective Inspector Pearce took the photo and shook her head and smiled. 'We already have that one, Kat,' she said. 'Along with sixty-four others. But thanks anyway.'

Aunt Gloria grabbed the photograph and peered at it. 'What is this?'

'It's a picture of the people in the pod, Aunt Gloria,' I explained. 'The pod that—'

'Not a trace of Salim in any of them, I'm afraid,' Detective Inspector Pearce said. 'Nor in the CCTV footage. I've been checking much of it myself. In that particular pod, a rather large gentleman –' she leaned over and pointed to the big white-haired man in the raincoat – 'stood in the same spot for nearly the whole ride and blocked much of the camera's view.'

Aunt Gloria tossed the picture down on the floor near my feet. I picked it up. 'You know what I think?' she said. 'I think he never went up that damn Wheel in the first place!'

'That's an interesting theory, Aunt Gloria,' I said, 'and one that I considered too, but—'

'Ted,' Mum said. She put a finger to her lip. That is body language even I have learned to read. It means 'Be quiet'.

There was another silence.

Then the inspector said she had a possible lead. A boy matching Salim's description had been seen at four o'clock yesterday afternoon by a guard at Euston Station, dodging the ticket barrier and getting on a train just a moment before the doors were locked.

'A train? What train?' Aunt Gloria said.

'An inter-city between London and Manchester.'

'Manchester? But that's where we'd just come from. Why would Salim go back there?'

'The boy – if it was Salim – was on his own. Unfortunately that's where we lose sight of him. The guard on the train has no memory of him. He could have got off at any of the stops in between. But the Manchester police are checking to see if Salim is perhaps in Manchester—'

'With his dad!' Aunt Gloria said.

'He is not with his father, I'm afraid. It was the first place we looked.' The inspector produced Salim's address book. 'We've spoken to everybody you told us he was close to. His cousins Ramesh and Yasmin. Your neighbours, the Tysons. His school friend, Marcus Flood. And his old friend from primary school, Paul Burridge.'

'And?'

'None of them say they've heard from him since you left the day before yesterday.'

'Hrumm,' I said. 'That's—'

'Hush, Ted,' said Mum.

'If Salim did go to Manchester,' Detective Inspector Pearce said to Aunt Gloria, 'where do you think he'd be most likely to go?'

Aunt Gloria stared into the space in front of her and then sighed. 'I don't think,' she said.

'Sorry?'

'I think the boy on the train is like the boy last night, the boy in the morgue. The boy you thought was Salim and wasn't.'

Detective Inspector Pearce reached over and touched Aunt Gloria's hand. 'I'm sincerely sorry about that, Gloria. We didn't have a proper photo ID then. We do now.' From a brown envelope she'd been holding she took out a photo of Salim and showed it to us. 'Your ex-husband gave us this. Would you say it's a good likeness?'

Salim was in a school blazer, with a sweatshirt underneath, and a faint line of a moustache over his lips. He was not looking either happy or sad in the photograph because his lips were straight, neither up nor down.

'That's him,' Aunt Gloria whispered. 'I bought

two copies so that Salim could give one to his father. To Rashid. I do it every year. I don't know why. I don't even know if Rashid has them framed. I don't—'

The doorbell rang. Dad went out into the hall to see who it was and I heard voices and then in walked a tall Indian man in jeans and a green shirt.

'Speak of the devil,' Aunt Gloria hissed. I only heard her say this because I was standing next to her. I didn't see anything particularly satanic about the strange man. I thought he must be another plain-clothes police officer. My hand flapped.

'What's this?' the man said. 'Have you found my son?' He looked at Aunt Gloria.

She looked at him. 'What are *you* doing here?'

'I'm looking for my son. What else? Trust you to lose him!'

Maybe Satan *had* entered the room after all because everybody started talking very loudly. I put my hands over my ears but I could still hear them. I counted the people in the room. Seven. I tried to guess the ages of those I didn't know. Then I added up the ages, actual or approximate, of all present. When I arrived at the figure of 233, and worked out the average age was 33.3 recurring, everyone was still shouting their heads off. The difference between laughing your head off and shouting your head off is that with one you are happy and with the other you are angry. I like it much better when people are laughing their heads off.

Detective Inspector Pearce got up from her chair. 'I'd better go,' she said, but I'm not sure that anyone listened except for me and Dad, who had not joined in the shouting either. Dad showed her out to the hallway and I followed. You could still hear the raised voices in the living room.

'Goodbye, Mr Spark,' Detective Inspector Pearce said. 'I'm sorry again about last night.'

I felt Dad's arm on my shoulder tighten. 'Will you find out who that poor boy was?'

'We're working on it,' Inspector Pearce said. 'And as for Salim, when everyone's calmed down, can you ask them if they would agree to us calling in the press?'

'The press?'

'Yes. If Salim's picture gets into the news stories, somebody who's seen him might come forward.'

Dad nodded. 'I'll ask them.'

'Inspector Pearce,' I said. My hand flapped. 'Salim got a call on his mobile yesterday. At approximately ten fifty a.m. He said it was from "a friend calling from Manchester to say goodbye".'

'Did he? How interesting.' She smiled at me, which meant she and I could be friends. 'If only some of my officers had half your brains, Ted.'

Then she nodded and walked down the tiny garden path to where the police car was parked.

Dad and I went back to the living room. Rashid was saying that the police had burst into his busy evening surgery last night and that all his patients must have thought he was another Dr Death, which was the name newspaper editors gave to a very evil doctor who killed dozens of his patients instead of making them better for no reason other than that he liked doing this. Aunt Gloria was clinging to a cushion as if she was about to throw it at him and saying that all he ever cared about was what other people thought about him. Mum was standing up and holding Kat by the elbow and ushering us back into the hallway.

She closed the living-room door behind her.

'God Almighty. Let's leave them to it,' she said. 'Let's go get a pizza, for pity's sake.'

So we did. Pity must have been pleased because we had four enormous pizzas at the pizza restaurant nearby. I had a Coca-Cola and Kat had Sprite and Mum had a beer and Dad had a bottle of sparkling water. Dad and I ate all of ours, and Mum and Kat swapped their last slice and left only bits of the crust, which meant that everybody had been extremely hungry. And over the meal we did not talk about Salim. I talked about thunderstorms and why they happen and Kat showed Dad how she had removed the silver nail polish from her hands and he said he was glad Cat-Woman had gone back to the moon.

When we got back, Rashid and Aunt Gloria were sitting on the sofa together arm in arm. This puzzled me until I remembered what Mum says about Kat and me having a love–hate relationship and I worked out that the same was true of Rashid and Aunt Gloria. Mum said to Rashid he was welcome to sleep on the couch if he wanted to and he said was she sure and she said she was and he said she was most kind and he would. And then Kat and I were told to go upstairs to bed, so we did.

TWENTY

Eavesdropping

Kat curled up on the lilo and went to sleep. The house went quiet.

Kat made a funny lapping noise, like a dog drinking water.

I couldn't sleep. I kept thinking of Salim, seeing his face with his lips turned up, fading in and out of the spokes of the London Eye. Then I remembered him saying I looked a cool dude and telling me that he got lonely. The boy on the slab. The boy on the train. Salim or not Salim.

I switched on the desk light. Kat didn't wake. She just moaned and turned over.

I got my weather-system book off my desk and looked at the photo of Kat and me on the bridge, as taken by Salim. I don't know much about photos, but I could see it was a good photo, not like the kind I take, because the lines around our faces were sharp, and we were exactly in the middle of the shot. A small strip of the Eye's wheel came up from my shoulder, with seven of the thirty-two pods shining in the sunlight.

I put the photo back in its hiding place, between the chapters on cyclones and anticyclones. I thought. Cyclones go anti-clockwise. Anticyclones go clockwise. That's if you're in the northern hemisphere. If you're in the southern hemisphere, it's the other way round. It's like water whirling down a plughole: in the northern hemisphere it whooshes anti-clockwise, in the south, clockwise.

And I realized that the same is true of the London Eye. I'd always thought of it as going anti-clockwise. If you look at it from the south bank of the river, that's how it goes. But (a big but) if you look at it from the north bank, it goes clockwise.

Whirlwinds and wheels: clockwise or anti-clockwise, depending on how you look at it. Nemotodes, such as earthworms: male or female, depending on how you look at it. Then there's Dad's favourite saying. A glass: half empty or half full, depending on how you look at it.

I scratched my head. *Depending on how you look at*

it – the same object can be or do opposite things at once. I remembered a picture Kat had once shown me of a waterfall. Only, the way it was painted, it looked as if the water was flowing upwards. Perhaps this was a clue to Salim's disappearance. Perhaps Kat and I were looking at things the wrong way up, or the wrong way round.

I got excited then, because I am good at looking at things differently. When I was little, I once drew an egg as three rings: the shell, the white and the yolk. It looked like the planet Saturn and the teacher at school said it was a very unusual way to draw an egg. She said I had drawn it in cross-section as if I had x-ray eyes and could see straight through it. I tried to look at Salim riding in his pod with x-ray eyes but I could only see figures in the pod, dark shadows, turning to have their souvenir photo taken.

So next I picked up the souvenir shot. After Aunt Gloria had tossed it on the floor earlier, and the police had said they didn't want it, I'd taken it back up to my desk. I studied the African women, the big white-haired man, the fat couple and their children,

the Japanese tourists. All I could see of the girl in the
pink jacket who'd stood near us in the queue was her
arm, waving at the camera above the other people. I
could not see her boyfriend, nor the tall blonde
woman with the grey-haired man who was shorter
than her. It had been a crowded pod. Not everyone
had fitted into the picture. Salim might have been at
the back somewhere, behind the shoulders and clut-
tered bodies. I tried to look in between the torsos
with x-ray eyes. But it was grey, murky shadow, tiny
dots, nothing more. I pushed it away.

I got up and crept downstairs to the kitchen. I
knew where Mum kept the salt and vinegar crisps
hidden and I needed some. I took two packets out
and crept back into the hallway. I paused. The
living-room door was ajar and I could hear Aunt
Gloria's voice. I decided to listen in case there was a
clue. Maybe Aunt Gloria knew something that she
didn't realize she knew but if I heard it I would be
able to see the significance. Mum has told me it is
wrong to eavesdrop on people. (Eavesdropping
is a strange word. Eaves are the parts of roofs that

project over the walls. The only thing that drops from them is rainwater and rainwater cannot hear.) Kat eavesdrops all the time. She lurks in the hallway when Mum and Dad are talking about serious matters such as school reports, and if I tell her it is wrong to do this, she hisses at me to get lost.

But tonight I decided to eavesdrop myself.

'I hate waiting,' Aunt Gloria was saying.

'I know you do.' It was Rashid. 'Patience and you – they don't go.'

'We should call in the press, Rashid. Like Inspector Pearce says.'

'Not yet, Gloria. I don't want our private affairs all over the place.'

'There you go again. Always caring about what other people think. What does it matter? What matters is Salim.'

'OK, Gloria. We'll call the press tomorrow. If Salim isn't found by then.'

There was a pause. I heard a groan and the sofa creaking.

'I'd do anything just to know Salim was alive, somewhere, anywhere, unharmed,' she said.

'He is, trust me. I feel it in my bones.'

'I hope your bones are right,' said Aunt Gloria. 'Oh, Rashid. If he comes back safe, let's be in touch more. It hasn't been good for him, our never talking.'

'Why are you taking him to New York, then? I nearly put an injunction on you.'

'You didn't!'

'I did. You never told me what you were planning. I only learned about it from Salim.'

'But I need the money, Rashid.'

'I pay you every month, don't I? As we agreed.'

'It's not enough. I need a good salary too.'

'Why? To pay for all your *clothes?*'

The voices were getting louder again. I edged backwards towards the stairs.

'You can rise as far up in your profession as you want,' Aunt Gloria said. 'Why can't *I*?'

'You're impossible, Gloria. You only ever think of yourself.'

'That's a lie. I'm the one who looks after Salim,

day in, day out. He's lived with me all his life. He's mine. He goes where I go.'

'Salim,' Rashid said, 'is Salim. He doesn't belong to either of us.'

There was a pause. I stood still. The sofa creaked again.

'You're right,' Aunt Gloria said. 'If anything happens to Salim, you say you'd never forgive me. But I'd never forgive myself.' Her voice wobbled, as if she was going to cry. I crept up the first stair.

'Don't blame yourself, Gloria,' Rashid said. Then I heard him groan. 'Salim asked me something the last time he visited me.'

'What?'

'He asked if he could come to live with me.'

'I don't believe it.'

'He did.'

'Never. Impossible.'

'I don't know if he meant it. But he did ask.'

'What did you say?'

'I said . . . that I was too busy every day at the surgery – that he was better off with his mother.

That he should go to New York, it was a fine city. I said no. I didn't even sit down and talk to him about it. He asked just as I was rushing out to a patient. I turned a deaf ear to him, Gloria.'

'Oh, Rashid! Don't you start. I can't stand to see grown men cry.'

Rustles, chokes, sighs. Then I guessed what came next. My hair stood on end. They were *kissing*. From the sound of it, it was the long-tongue-like-eels kind that Kat told me about a couple of years back. She says that they do it in the movies, when their cheeks move about. That they do it in the school corridors when the teachers aren't looking. That Mum and Dad do it when we're not looking.

My mum threatens us with weird punishments sometimes. If I forget to change my school shirt three days running, she'll yank it off me, screech at the state of the collar and threaten to hang me on the washing line by my toenails if I forget to change it next time. She's joking, you realize. But if you were to ask me, what would I prefer – being hung from a washing line by my toenails, or having to be kissed by somebody like Aunt Gloria – I know which I would choose. The washing line, every time.

I fled upstairs as fast as I could. I'd had enough eavesdropping for one night.

TWENTY-ONE

Mix and Match

I got back into bed, careful not to wake Kat. I munched on my crisps, letting them soften in my mouth before I bit into them so as to make less noise. Quietly I got out the list of theories and the photos. I thought. I bunched up the washing-line photos and put them on the desk. Then I went through the others. I finished one packet of crisps and opened a second.

Halfway through the packet I stopped munching and stared. I looked at another shot and stared at that too.

'Kat!' I hissed. I shook her shoulder hard.

She raised herself from the pillow, holding her head between her hands. 'Ugh. What a dream. What is it?' She blinked up at me from the lilo.

'The strange man, Kat,' I said. 'The man who sold us the ticket.'

She shook her head. 'Yyyeerggg,' she yawned.

(That is what it sounded like.) 'What about him?'

'I've found him!' I squeaked.

Kat's eyes went round and she looked confused. So I showed her the photo that I had taken, the one that had gone wrong, with the headless bodies. I pointed to a torso of a man, with a jacket flapping over a T-shirt.

'That's him!' I said.

'How do you know? He just looks like someone in a crowd. And anyway, what's he got to do with it?'

'Maybe nothing. Maybe everything.'

Kat put her head to one side like I do sometimes, because it helps you to think. My theory is that it allows blood to pour into the side of the brain you need for whatever bit of thinking it is you have to do. The right-hand side is for logical deduction and analytical thinking and the left-hand side is for creative thought, and I think it is from this side that inspiration comes from.

'It was odd the way he came up to us,' Kat said. 'You could say, suspicious. Or maybe just coincidence.' She picked up the picture and looked at it again. 'Don't say you remember him just from that. You never notice what people wear.'

'No. Not from that picture on its own, Kat. But look at this one too.' I showed her the photo taken just before, by Salim. Salim had snapped one of the Eye, but lopped the top part off, because he was too close. In the foreground was part of the queue and various bystanders. When you looked really hard at the individual people in it, you could see the head and shoulders of a man, facing towards the camera. It was only the size of a pea, but enough of the face was recognizable.

'That's him,' I said.

Kat looked hard. 'You're right, Ted. It *is* him.' She took the other photo. 'That's his head and shoulders. And this is his chest and trousers. They match.'

I got a magnifying glass out of my desk drawer. We looked at the pictures together. It was a game of mix and match, head and tail. Fitting together things that belonged. A jigsaw.

'There's something written on his T-shirt,' Kat said, peering through the glass. 'Can't make it out. An O and a T for sure. The rest's blurred.' She looked at me. 'You know, Ted, this might be a break-through.' She clapped me on the shoulder so hard I coughed. 'Tomorrow I'm going back to the photo shop with the negatives. I'm going to ask them to blow up the two shots. But Ted – don't say anything to anyone about this.'

'What about Mum and—?'

'She'd only ignore us if we tried to explain. No. I'm following up this lead on my own.'

'Not on your own, Kat.'

She clapped me on the shoulder again. 'With you, Ted. Of course. We'll figure out what it says on the T-shirt. And maybe, just maybe, we'll track him down.'

I was so excited I forgot to *hrumm*.

'Ted – can't stand to say it, but you're a genius.'

Then she grabbed the packet of crisps I'd been eating and scoffed the lot.

TWENTY-TWO

Word Game

We slept for what was left of that night. When I woke up, freshening winds had moved in from the west. Light rain pattered on the window. The lilo on the floor was empty. I imagined where the clue of the strange man with the ticket might lead and how it might fit in with the theories left on the list. *Depending on how you look at it.* I remembered my thoughts from the night before, about how things can go clockwise and anti-clockwise at the same time. There was a tangle in my head.

Kat came in, wriggling into her fur-collared jacket. It was tight for her. First one arm then another went up into the air as she squeezed into the sleeves. 'I'm off, Ted,' she whispered. 'To get the photos blown up before anyone notices. Back in an hour.'

She put a finger to her lips, picked up the photo packet containing the negatives and went out.

I looked across at my desk. The photos of the

clothes on the washing line were scattered over it and I could see jumbled images of Dad's tartan shirt, pinned up by the shoulders and cuffs, and Mum's black long-sleeved T-shirt upside down and Kat's school sweatshirt and Dad's boxer shorts and three of Mum's bras and my pyjamas. I put the photos into a tidy pile and lay back on my pillow. The cool air from a front across London fanned my forehead. I imagined the weather satellite picture – a jumble of patchy cloud, looking like the jumble in my brain.

That's what I need, I thought. A bird's-eye view, from a satellite. A geo-stationary satellite, 36,000 kilometres above the earth, can beam down images in seconds. It measures the heat of the clouds and the surface temperature of the sea. It tells meteorologists what's happening and can help them to understand the approaching weather systems and make predictions.

Then I remembered: even a geo-stationary satellite can be two things at once, still or moving. It stays in the same place in relation to the earth's surface, but only because it orbits at the same speed as the earth's spin. Clockwise or anti-clockwise, male or female, half empty or half full, stationary or moving, *depending on how you look at it.*

I groaned and dug my head with its swirling brain waves under the pillow. Mum and Aunt Gloria's voices called up and down the stairs. There was no sound of Dad's voice. My clock said 9.02, which meant he had gone to work. Then Rashid's voice came up from the kitchen. I smelled toast.

An hour went by. I got dressed. I put on the shirt I'd worn the day before and the day before that, but I didn't think Mum would notice. At 10.05 I crept out onto the landing just as Kat's shape appeared through the frosted glass of the front door. It opened slowly. Kat was sneaking in with her key. She saw me at the top of the stairs and put her finger to her mouth again. But Mum must have heard her. She appeared from the kitchen before Kat could get up the stairs.

'Where've you been, Kat? I didn't say you could wander out when you felt like it.'

'Hi, Kat,' I said. 'Did you get it?'

Kat stared at Mum then at me.

'My compass,' I said. I went downstairs and tapped Mum on the elbow. 'I think it dropped out of my pocket yesterday. Kat said she'd have a look in the front garden for me.'

'Oh,' Mum said. She ruffled my head. 'I didn't know you'd lost it. Sorry, Kat. I thought you'd gone off somewhere. *Did* you get it?'

'No,' Kat said. 'I hunted around the bushes. Nothing.'

'It was only a cheap one,' I said. 'But good at tracking the wind direction.'

'Maybe,' Mum said, 'when all this is over' – she paused and shook her head – '*if* all this is ever over, we'll get you a new one. And something for Kat too. If you both stay quiet and calm while all this—'

She stopped, shrugged, shook her head and returned to the kitchen. Kat looked at me. I looked at her.

'Go, Ted,' Kat whispered. She punched me in the arm so hard I nearly fell down the stairs. 'Never thought I'd see the day. You *lied*.'

We went upstairs to my room and Kat took out a large card envelope that had been stuffed up her front. 'The man in the shop . . .' she said. 'He knows me now. He blew up the pictures for me in less than an hour. Here they are.'

She ripped the seal and took out two large prints. One was of the strange man who'd sold us the ticket. His face was blurred but recognizable, with his stubbly chin, dark eyebrows and high forehead. He squinted into the light.

The other was of three torsos, but the middle one was his. You could recognize a shabby leather jacket, a hairy neck, a black T-shirt or sweatshirt, and his fingers with a roll-up cigarette in them. The jacket was open and flapping. We could see some of what was written on the shirt in white lettering:

ONTLI
ECUR

The beginnings and ends of each of the two words were cut off by the jacket.

'A word game,' Kat murmured. She sat at my desk and grabbed a piece of paper. 'We have to find out what words have those letters in the middle.' She copied out the letters and looked at them. 'To the right of the I – do you see, Ted? There's a downward stroke, and then a bit of a diagonal – perhaps an N?

I considered the alphabet in capital letters. 'Could be an M.'

'Maybe – but somehow I think it's an N.' She tapped her pencil. I heard her muttering: 'BONT – CONT – DONT – EONT . . .' and so on until she came to 'ZONT'. Then she threw down the pencil.

'Hopeless,' she said.

'What about the second word?' I said. 'Maybe it's *recurring?*' I thought of 'recurring' because my favourite number is 3.3 recurring. I like the way the point 3s go off into infinity, like a chain of Gods.

'*Recurring* – hey, that would fit.' She wrote down the word and muttered it under her breath. She looked at the word in silence. 'You know, Ted, I've been having one,' she said.

'What?'

'A recurring nightmare. Every night since Salim . . . went.'

'What happens in it?'

She shut her eyes. 'First I'm in a morgue. And there's this boy lying on a slab and I'm too frightened to look at his face, Ted. Then suddenly I'm in a pod on the Eye. It's turning fast – faster than it really does. It speeds up. I'm looking out. I can't see anything. It's foggy, a white mist everywhere. Then the Eye stops. At the very top. It stops. And the glass . . .'

'What?'

'The glass dissolves, Ted. And I'm falling – falling through the white spokes. Like through a cat's cradle. And the fog . . . I can't see where I'm going to land . . .' Her hand went to her throat.

'A dream, Kat,' I said.

She shook herself. 'Yeah. I know.' She looked at the letters and sighed. 'If it was RECURRING the R-I-N-G would go too far to the right. The G would be under the armpit.' She rapped the pencil on her knuckle. 'Why do people have words on clothes, Ted?'

'I don't know,' I said. 'It looks funny, people walking around like signposts, or billboard adverts.'

'It's not my idea of style. Especially those joke T-shirts, like FRAGILE GOODS: HANDLE WITH CARE.' She grinned. 'I saw that the other day on a lady with the most enormous . . .' She cupped her arms in front of her chest.

'Hrumm,' I said.

'Telling me. But I don't think this is a joke T-shirt. It's only two words.'

'You get ones with names of universities,' I remembered.

'So you do – but probably not,' she said. 'There'd be a crest or something. A design or motto to go with the college name.'

'If it *is* a college, would it help knowing it?'

'How d'you mean?'

'You can buy those sweatshirts anywhere. You might be anybody. There's this boy in my class. He has a sweatshirt that says OXFORD UNIVERSITY. But he's too young to go to Oxford, isn't he?'

Kat's head went into her hands. She groaned. 'This is a waste of time.'

'On the other hand,' I continued, 'there's this other boy whose mum picks him up from school and she wears a T-shirt with GARDENS FOR THE DISABLED on it. The letters circle around a big daisy. And it's the organization where she works.'

Kat's head came up. 'True,' she said. 'ONTLI ECUR,' she muttered. 'Is it where he works – or a club or a society? Something he's part of? Something that just might lead us to him?' She looked at the fuzzy torso, the faded white letters. She leaped up like a jack-in-the-box.

'*Security!*' she yelled.

'Sorry?'

'The second word, dumbo! It's *security*.'

My head went off to one side.

'He works in security.'

'Security,' I agreed. I was impressed and disappointed at the same time that I hadn't seen the word before Kat. 'What about the first word?'

Kat sat down again, frowning in concentration.

'ONTLI . . . ONTLI . . .' she muttered like a mantra.

'Kat,' I said, 'there's something I don't understand. About photos.'

'Shush,' she said and continued the mantra.

'Why aren't the letters the wrong way round, Kat?'

'Hey?'

'You know. When you take a photo. Why don't letters appear back to front, like in a mirror image.'

She didn't answer. 'ontli . . . ONTLI . . .' she went. Then she stopped. 'What did you say?'

'I said – why aren't the letters—?'

I stopped. Kat was staring at me, her eyes large and round, her mouth open.

'Sorry, sorry, Kat, I didn't mean to put you off . . .'

'No, no—' she began. But what she was about to say was cut off by an ear-piercing screech from downstairs.

TWENTY-THREE

Katastrophe

The shriek had come from the kitchen. Kat gasped and gripped my arm hard. Then she ran from the room and pounded downstairs. I followed her as fast as I could. I wondered whether somebody had been murdered. It sounded like the kind of scream you get on old-fashioned TV detective stories, when the maid goes in with a tray and finds a dead body and drops the tray and makes an ear-piercing noise. An image of Aunt Gloria finding Salim dead in the cellar went through my head and a bad feeling went up my oesophagus.

Kat stopped in the kitchen doorway. I peered over her shoulder to see what was happening beyond. Mum, Aunt Gloria and Rashid were standing at the table, staring at Aunt Gloria's mobile phone.

'What's happened?' Kat said.

Nobody replied. It was as if we'd come upon a game of statues. Kat walked over to the table and reached over to pick up the mobile.

'Don't touch it!' Aunt Gloria whispered.

Kat's hand paused. 'Why not?'

Mum pushed Kat's hand away. 'Just stay out of this, Kat. Can't you see Glo's upset?'

Rashid's hands went up palm outwards. 'Come, come, let's sit down, calm down,' he said. 'Let's get to the bottom of this.'

Everybody obeyed except me (there were only four chairs). I stood by Mum's shoulder.

'Gloria,' Rashid soothed. He took her hand and stroked it like you would a cat. 'Tell us what happened.'

Aunt Gloria swallowed. 'I've been carrying my mobile with me everywhere. Never losing sight of it. It's been by the pillow. In my pocket. In my hand. All the time. Just in case Salim should call. Then – just now— Oh!' She wiped a tear off her cheek. 'For two minutes I put it here, on the table, while I went into the living room. To call the airline. From the landline. I had to call the airline, you see. Because, by rights' – she shook her head and her lips squashed up together – 'by rights, today, we should be flying across the Atlantic, Salim and I. And I rang them to explain why we won't make the flight. And the lady on the phone was very kind.'

Her lips went one way, her nose another and her eyes disappeared altogether. She was crying. I couldn't see why someone being kind should make Aunt Gloria cry, but it did. 'She said she'd hold our reservations. That's if Salim . . . is found. They'll put us on the first available flight to New York. So I said thank you. And I hung up. I put the phone back. And I came back in here. And *it* was ringing. The mobile. It was on the table, ringing and ringing, and nobody was in here, nobody to hear it. I picked it up, answered it – and it rang off . . .'

'It could have been anyone,' Rashid said.

Aunt Gloria shook her head. She picked up the phone and showed us its display panel. The name of the last caller was displayed.

Salim.

'He tried to call me . . . I called back, of course. Right away. But nobody picked up. It was switched off again. Nobody. Oh, Salim. You called me. And I wasn't there for you.'

The last six words came out in a wail that grew louder until the 'you'. Then she got stuck on the 'oo' sound.

'Oo-oo-oooo,' she cried, like a baby that's dropped its bottle.

Viking North Utsire South Utsire Forties cyclonic six to gale eight, I chanted in my head. *Decreasing five, rough or very rough.*

'Oh, Glo,' Mum said. She took her by the elbow and they went to stand out in the back garden and I saw Mum handing Aunt Gloria her packet of cigarettes and her lighter, which was very strange because my mother is a nurse and nurses know all about how smoking is hazardous for human health. Aunt Gloria would have been better off with a cup of tea because in my book of first aid it says a hot drink is good for you if you have had a shock.

Rashid sat slumped at the kitchen table. He put his head in his hands and muttered something about calling in the press. Then he went out into the garden too.

Kat looked at me. 'Ted,' she said, 'this is getting serious.'

'Serious,' I agreed.

She got up from the table and walked around it three times until I felt dizzy. I could see she was thinking. When Kat thinks, she moves about a lot, but when I think, apart from putting my head to one side, I am still. I didn't like the way Kat was think-ing. Her ponytail swung from one side to the other and her lips were pressed up tight and her mouth was moving but no sound came out. Suddenly she went into the living room. I followed her. She picked up the A–Z phone book from the shelf and flicked through it with her eyebrows pulled together. Then she turned a page over and nodded. She tore out the page and folded it.

'Ted,' she said, 'I'm going out. This instant.'

'But . . .'

'You're just going to have to lie again. Say I've gone round to Tiff's.' Tiffany is Kat's best friend at school.

'But you're not going to Tiffany's, are you?' I said.

'No,' she said.

'Hrumm.'

'Stop twitching your head like that! All you have to say if Mum asks is that I've popped over to Tiff's. Got it?'

'Popped over to Tiff's.'

'For the afternoon.'

'For the afternoon.'

'Don't drone it like that. Say it like you mean it, Ted.'

'But I don't mean it, Kat. It's not true.'

Kat slapped her forehead. 'How did I end up with a brother like you? How? You're a hopeless case.'

'Where are you really going, Kat?'

'If I tell you, you'll tell the others.'

'I won't, Kat. Not if they don't ask me.'

'They *will* ask you. There's no time to lose. I've got to check this thing out myself.'

'No,' I said. 'No, Kat.'

She was in the hall, putting on her jacket.

'No,' I said.

She ran upstairs to fetch her leopard-skin back-pack. I followed her. She stuffed the blown-up photo of the strange man's blurry face into it along with the phonebook page and ran downstairs again.

'No,' I said, following. My hand shook itself out. 'No, Kat.'

'I'll be back as soon as I can.'

'Kat!'

She opened the front door.

'Kat!' I grabbed the sleeve of her jacket. 'Take me with you. Please.'

'Gerroff, Ted,' she said. She tried to slap my hand away.

'Uh-uh-uh,' I grunted. I held on.

'Let go, Ted.' She shoved me hard back through the front door. 'I'm sorry, Ted. You're really good at thinking. But you're no good at doing. If you come with me, you won't be any use.'

She slammed the door in my face. I saw her silhouette go down the path. I slumped to the hall carpet and a feeling like molten magma churned in my belly. My foot banged up against the skirting board, my hand shook itself out and my brain went into a whirling vortex of bad feelings. Katastrophe. Kataclysm. Katalogue of Disasters. Hurricane Katrina. Mean, mad, mad, mean Kat.

TWENTY-FOUR

Bingo

I went upstairs before Mum and the others found me. I didn't want to have to explain anything. I didn't want to have to tell the Tiffany lie. But first I fetched the phonebook. I wanted to find out which page Kat had torn out.

You would think that would be easy but it wasn't. The *Business and Services Book* for London has 989 pages. The pages are floppy and thin. When one page is missing, it doesn't automatically open on that page. You have to search page by page until you see a break in the page numbering at the top.

I started at the beginning, with businesses that are called things with number-beginnings, like '00 Finance'. By page 6 you are on the As. By page 75 you are on the Bs. By 'Eye of the Needle Software Solutions' my own eyes were like needles and my fingers were black. The pages rubbed against my finger-pads like cotton wool as I turned them. Sweat trickled down my neck. The cool breeze of the morning had gone. The temperature was climbing. Downstairs, I heard the police arrive.

I started on the Fs. By *Family to Fashion* I was beginning to wonder about going the other way: starting on the Zs and working backwards. But I'd seen Kat hunting through the book and I'd had the impression she'd been looking nearer the start. Then I remembered about mirrors. I picked up the book and rifled through it the way Kat had done, but in front of the mirror on my wardrobe door. Mirror image, the other way round, back to front . . . *depending on how you look at it* . . . I remembered Kat staring at me after I'd asked her about why letters in photos appear the right way round and not back to front.

Then I dropped the phone book. ONT – FRONT.

My favourite weather word. Why hadn't I thought of it sooner?

I skipped forward through *Fashion, Felt, Fisher, Flowers, Fortune.* Sure enough, page 333/334 was missing, as were all entries between 'Frocks Galore' and 'Futon Futura'.

The rest was easy.

ONTLI ECUR. FRONTLINE SECURITY.

I said out loud what Dad says whenever he finishes the weekend crossword.

Bingo.

TWENTY-FIVE

The TV Crew

I went downstairs. I had worked out what Kat had worked out and I was glad. But now I needed to think some more. What was the next thing to do? The police were in the kitchen. The door was open. I did some more eavesdropping and heard Detective Inspector Pearce saying, 'It could have been anyone phoning, Gloria. Not necessarily Salim. Anyone who had found or borrowed his phone.'

And then another police officer: 'Sometimes mobile phones ring a number of their own accord – when the keypad's not locked.'

It wasn't very interesting, and while the grown-ups' attention was diverted, I decided it was a good time to take action.

I crept into the living room and picked up the phone. One thing I know about, because Mum has shown me, is getting an unknown number through Directory Enquiries. The six numbers to dial are in my head. I dialled them and a man answered.

'Frontline Security,' I said. 'London.'

He put me through to an automatic voice, which gave me an eleven-digit number. I memorized it.

I hung up and dialled the number.

There was music playing and then a recorded message:

'Welcome to Frontline Security, the number one London security company. We supply stewards, ticket collectors, body-searchers and guards with two-way radios. Whether you're hosting a celebrity party, a firework show, a popular concert or an exhibition, we can meet all your requirements. Frontline Security. Your complete security solution. Please hold while we put you through to an operator.'

The music started again. My free hand flapped. I was still waiting for the 'operator' when Rashid came in. I wondered if I should put the phone down but he smiled at me and said nothing. He fetched his jacket from the back of the armchair and left the room. I was still on hold. The recorded announcement went round another time, then another. Halfway through the fourth time there was a click and a real woman's voice saying, 'Hello-Frontline-Security-can-I-help-you?'

'Hrumm,' I said.

'Hello?' the woman said again.

I didn't know what to say.

'Hello?'

My mind spun like the vortex of a tropical cyclone.

'Hello? Is anybody there? Frontline Security?'

I hung up.

Just as I did so, I heard a big van draw up outside. Doors slammed, voices shouted, the doorbell rang. I looked out of the window. A television crew had arrived. Aunt Gloria and Rashid had decided to go public.

Within minutes, the house was full of men in jeans and trainers, carrying cables, cameras, light stands, microphones. The living room was very busy indeed. Sometimes when Dad asks Mum how work was, she says the ward was like Piccadilly Circus. I imagine flashing lights and people bumping into each other and drug trolleys zooming around like fast cars and that's how it was in our living room now. Nobody noticed me standing by the telephone. Detective Inspector Pearce talked on her mobile. Aunt Gloria searched her make-up bag. Mum helped a cameraman plug a camera light into the socket behind the sofa. She looked up and saw me.

'Ted. There you are. Where's Kat?'

My mouth opened but no words came out. Instead the cameraman said, 'Pass the plug over, love,' and Mum was distracted. Seconds later a man with a thin, frowning face said, 'Let's roll.' But instead of rolling, another man said, 'Lights. Camera. Action. Take one.'

Aunt Gloria sat on the sofa. Rashid sat next to her. She'd put on some bright orange lipstick and this made her face look whiter than usual and the skin between her eyelashes and eyebrows looked bruised.

'This is a message,' she began. She swallowed, took Rashid's hand. 'A message. If you are holding Salim – if you know where my boy is – if you think you might have seen him, please, please come forward. We'll do anything to have him back. He's our boy. Just a call to let us know he's safe. To let us know he's . . . alive.' Her face crumpled. 'The worry is crippling us. *Please*. Call the police. Thank you.'

'Cut,' the thin-faced man said to the cameraman. 'That was great, missis,' he said to Aunt Gloria.

'Do you want me to do it again?' Aunt Gloria said. 'Do you want another take?'

'No need, love.'

'Are you sure?'

'Fine first time. You're a natural.'

And within minutes the camera crew had packed up and left. Mum and Rashid saw them out to their van and the police left at the same time. This meant I was on my own in the room with Aunt Gloria. She sat on the sofa staring into space.

'Oh, Ted,' she said after a minute of silence. She was looking straight at me and I couldn't understand what her expression meant. I thought she was going to say something cross. But instead she shook her head and her eyes watered. 'Did I do all right?' she whispered.

'Yes, Aunt Gloria,' I said.

'Do you think somebody out there might hear, might help?'

'It's a possibility,' I said.

'What do you think, Ted? Do *you* think Salim is all right?'

'Hrumm,' I said.

'What does *that* mean?' she said. Her face took on its mini ice-age look.

'I was just thinking, Aunt Gloria.'

The mini ice age thawed. She sighed. Her hand went out and landed on my head. She ruffled my hair the way Mum does. I squirmed. Aunt Gloria didn't notice.

'You know, Ted, I'm sick to my stomach.'

I stared at her stomach in confusion.

'At least you're honest,' she said. 'Everyone keeps telling me he's OK, they're sure he's fine, it will all work out, he'll be back any minute. But minute after minute goes by and he isn't back. They don't mean what they say. The truth is, we just don't know.'

'Aunt Gloria,' I said, 'Salim has to be somewhere.

It's a mystery. I'm working on it. In my brain.'

'Your brain,' Aunt Gloria repeated. She smiled at me, but it reminded me of the way Mum smiled at me the time I asked her about miracle cures and whether I could get one for my syndrome if I prayed hard enough. Like Mum's then, Aunt Gloria's lips turned up but at the same time a tear came down her cheek. She took my hand and rubbed my knuckles, which was a strange thing to do and started my other hand flapping. 'Sometimes I think there's more in that brain of yours, Ted, than in the rest of ours put together. If brains alone could bring Salim back, yours would do it.'

Then Aunt Gloria got up from the sofa and went upstairs to Kat's room, which was where she was sleeping.

I didn't want to run into Mum in case she asked me about Kat again and I would have to tell the Tiffany lie. So I went where I always go when I want to do my two favourite things, think and watch the weather: the back garden.

The shirts were still flapping on the line. They

had been up for three days. Mum had forgotten about them. I touched them. They were damp from the light rain we'd had that morning. I paced the lawn to check it hadn't grown or shrunk. Twelve-and-a-half strides wide and seven across, the same as last week. Then I realized that when I grew taller, and my legs longer, the number of strides would decrease. It was another example of how things can change, depending on how you look at them. I was back with the water going down the plughole in different directions, depending on which hemisphere you were in; the London Eye revolving in different directions depending on which side of the river you were on; worms being male and female; satellites moving and staying still. Something flickered in my brain. It was a pattern – two things that looked alike; something that looked like one thing but was really another thing. I pinched my right forearm to make the pattern stay, but it didn't. It vanished before I could fix it, before I could find out what it was.

I looked up at the sky. Thin strata cloud, white and harmless, floated in the southeast. But to the northwest, in the heart of the city, a cumulus cloud was in formation. I stared as vapour collected and imagined how the particles of water were swirling around a central funnel, making it into a threatening shaft. It might or might not bring rain. It was moving this way over the skyline. Its heavy bulbous shape billowed out as rising air currents added to its mass.

I thought of Kat, out there, somewhere in the city, under the growing cumulus cloud, on the trail of the strange man who sold us the ticket. And I knew what I had to do.

I got to the phone in Mum and Dad's bedroom with nobody noticing. I dialled Frontline Security again.

'Frontline Security?' came the same female voice after the music and the recorded announcement.

'Hello,' I said.

'Hello,' she said. 'Can I help you?'

'Hrumm,' I said.

'Sorry,' she said. 'Didn't catch that.'

'Er,' I said.

'You're just a kid, aren't you?'

'I am twelve years old,' I said.

'Well,' she said, 'I'm just a temp.'

There was a silence. I thought hard.

'Have you got the right number?' she asked.

'Yes.'

'So who're you looking for?'

'A man,' I said.

'A man?'

'A man with a stubbly chin.'

She laughed loudly. 'Sounds like Christy. He's the only one here who never shaves properly. You're the second person who's been after him today. I'll tell you what I told her. He's not here.'

'Not here.'

'*I'm* the only one here today.'

'Oh.'

'I *manning* the phone. So to speak.' She laughed some more down the phone. I didn't understand the joke but I did what Mr Shepherd told me to and laughed as well.

'First it's a young girl who's looking for the friend

of her older brother – she's got a picture of him, but she doesn't know what he's called, and she's desperate, because he's left his asthma inhaler in her house. Now it's a kid looking for a man with a stubbly chin. Well, honey, I'll tell you what I told the girl. It's no skin off my teeth.'

I pictured the pink flesh around her molars.

'Christy's with the other guys and girls. They're all on the same job this week. Down Earl's Court at the Motorcycle and Scooter Show.'

'Earl's Court?'

'The big exhibition hall. If you find Christy there, don't say I told you, will you?'

'No,' I said. But she'd already hung up.

You can live a whole life, twelve years and 188 days (or 4,571 days, not forgetting the three extra days for the leap years), and not tell a single lie. Then on day 4,572 you tell two. The first lie I told was about the lost compass that wasn't really lost. The second lie was the note I wrote and left by the phone. It said,

Dear Mum,
We have gone swimming to get some exercise. Ted.

Next I took fifteen one-pound coins from the treasure chest that I've had since I was five. I went to the end of the landing and listened. Mum and Rashid were downstairs in the kitchen again. They were talking quietly. The house was calm.

I crept down the stairs. I headed for the front door. I opened it, stepped out into the sunshine and paused. Was this the right thing to do? What if Mum found the note and didn't believe it? What if I didn't find Kat in Earl's Court Exhibition Centre? What if I didn't find Earl's Court at all? What if I didn't even make it to our local underground station?

But Kat-astrophe, Kat-aclysm, Kat-alogue of Disasters, my mean, mad sister, wasn't going to leave me behind, not when so much was at stake. I inched the door shut. I headed out through our postage-stamp front garden. I closed the gate behind me and walked out onto the pavement and down the road.

TWENTY-SIX

The Coriolis Effect

As I walked, I thought about how tracking things down is very hard. Tracking the weather is one of the most difficult things of all. You can spot a hurricane as it crosses the ocean, but not know the exact path it will take or when and where it will hit land. There are too many variables that alter its course. Such as the Coriolis effect.

The Coriolis effect is very interesting. You can't see the Coriolis effect, you can't touch it, but it exists. It deflects things. It's a powerful force in the world. This is how it works.

As you know, the earth rotates. If you're standing on the equator, you rotate with it, 40,000 kilometres in twenty-four hours. You're going at 1,670 kilometres an hour, but you feel like you're standing still. The speed that you don't realize you are doing is your tangential velocity. But if you stand on the North Pole, you don't go any distance at all. You go round on the spot. Your tangential velocity is zero.

The Coriolis effect happens because of the difference between these two tangential velocities. If you throw something from the equator towards the North Pole, it won't go straight, but crooked. The difference in tangential velocities deflects or distorts it. Your missile lands a little to the right. But if you were standing on the equator, and launched a missile to the south, it would land to the left, not the right. Right in the northern hemisphere, left in the southern hemisphere. It is like the different directions of the water swirling down the plughole.

As I walked away from our house, I thought about the Coriolis effect. I thought about Salim's disappearance. Perhaps tracking Salim was like tracking the weather – only without knowing about the Coriolis effect. We didn't know what had deflected him off his course. But something had.

I thought about distortion, deflection, whirlwinds and weather. I thought about north, south, male, female, full, empty, anti-clockwise, clockwise. I stopped on a corner. I realized I had gone the wrong way and wasn't sure where I was.

I'm a dyslexic geographer. I forget my left from my right. My hand was shaking itself out, until I looked up and saw the cumulus cloud I'd noticed earlier. It had grown into a cumulonimbus. It hung down from a glowering sky behind London's tower blocks. Rain or hail, possibly thunder, approached. I headed back in the direction I'd come from, back past our house, and towards the cloud. Somehow it felt correct. Sure enough, soon I was out on the main road and from there I could see the underground station.

Being a dyslexic geographer, I can't read maps. I never know if I should read them upright or upside down. But there's one map I can read, which is the one of the London Underground. Because it's a topological map, you are in a universe where the spaces between points don't matter and all that counts is the sequence of stops and where the lines cross. You could stretch the tube map into all sorts of hoops and loops and it would be the same map, as long as the junctions were the same.

I stood at the tube map for a very long time.

Then I found Earl's Court. It was on the green line and on the blue line.

This meant I had to get the black line to Embankment and change onto the green line or take the black line to Leicester Square and change onto the blue line. I decided the Embankment route was shorter.

I bought a travel card and went down to the platform.

I put my hand in my jacket pocket to stop it from shaking itself out.

The sign said a train to High Barnet via Charing Cross was due. I heard a rumble in the tunnel and then the train came into the station like a silver streak of lava pouring down a volcano. The doors opened. I went in and took a seat.

The carriage was half full, or half empty, depending on how you looked at it.

Some graffiti was scratched onto the glass window opposite: NO WAY. It was razor-etched, with slashing parallel white lines for each stroke of every letter. This was a bad thing somebody had done just for the sake of it, like why Dr Death killed his patients.

A bad feeling started in my oesophagus.

Usually when I get the tube I am with Kat and Mum and sometimes Dad. I like to tell them in advance what the next stop is, which shows how well I can read the map, and I also say how many more stops we have to go. But they were not with me. So I counted the stations and said their names in my head. That way, I wouldn't forget to get off when I had to.

Between Waterloo and Embankment the trains go under the Thames. It is a long stop. I saw a man staring hard at an advertisement for car insurance. He was sitting under the graffiti sign and his eyebrows were close together. There were lines on his forehead and his lips were pressed together, which meant he was angry. He also had a plaster on his cheek.

I remembered how Sherlock Holmes once amazed Watson by working out Watson's train of thought. (A train of thought is a good way to describe someone's series of connected thoughts, because they are attached to each other like carriages are by couplers.) Holmes did this by watching Watson's face and the things he was staring at and making deductions.

So I worked out that the man opposite me was having a train of thought about a car crash he had had, which was why he had an injury, and that the advertisement for car insurance made him angry because he had not been insured.

I was so pleased with this piece of deductive thinking that I nearly forgot to get out when the train stopped.

A woman's voice announced, '*This station is Embankment. Please take care when leaving the train as there is a gap between the train and the station platform.*' I jumped up with my hand flapping and only just made it through the doors before they closed. Then I nearly fell down the gap but didn't.

I followed the signs for the green line, westbound. I got a train that said EALING BROADWAY on the front. I had seven stops to go. It was a brighter journey, closer to the surface. I could see flashes of daylight. I could smell damp. I didn't try to work out what any of my fellow passengers were thinking but kept concentrating on the order of stops, and at Earl's Court I got out.

The weather had changed. Hail was bouncing off the corrugated station roof. Hail is a shower of irregular lumps of ice and always comes from cumulonimbus clouds, so I knew I was right under the cloud I'd seen forming earlier. Judging by the sound, these stones might be ten to fifteen milli-metres wide. I went through the ticket barrier. I stood in the ticket hall, blinking at the signs for different exits.

A station guard came over. 'Hey,' he said. 'You, boy. Are you lost?'

I considered whether or not I should speak to him. Everyone knows you are not supposed to speak to strangers. We'd spoken to the strange man at the London Eye and perhaps that was why we were in such trouble. But this man was in a London Underground uniform and this meant it was his job to help lost passengers.

'Yes,' I said.

'Where are you going?' he said.

'Earl's Court,' I said.

'This *is* Earl's Court,' he said. 'Maybe you're after the exhibition centre?'

'The exhibition centre,' I agreed.

'Go up those stairs. Keep straight on through to the tube exit and it's opposite. Huge. You can't miss it,' he said. He didn't once say go left, go right; he just pointed in the right direction.

Perhaps he was a dyslexic geographer too.

'Remember to duck the hail,' he called after me.

Perhaps he was a meteorologist too.

I made my way up the station stairs, veering slightly to the right as I did so. This was because I was imagining that I was a missile, being hurled from the equator into the northern hemisphere. So the amount that I veered was equal to the deflection caused by the Coriolis force. And this made me feel good.

TWENTY-SEVEN

Biker Hell

Through bouncing hail, which was on average about twelve millimetres in diameter, across a busy road, loomed a big building with a banner plastered over it: MOTORCYCLE AND SCOOTER SHOW. The hailstones died away, the last globules tapping my head and shoulders as I crossed over. Inside the main entrance, people were crushed up together. There was a 'person-counter' by the ticket desk registering the daily numbers. Today's figure was 19,997 and rising.

I'd never seen such a crowd. It was mostly men in black leathers, with silver studs and black glossy orbs – helmets – on their head or under their arm. I felt as if I had been beamed from earth onto an intergalactic space station. Were they men or clones? They laughed, argued and shouted. I wasn't sure about them. They looked like the rough boys in our school who go round in gangs and if you come up against them in the corridor you had better turn and run away. These men seemed worse than those boys. But they didn't spit at me or elbow me in the ribs or call me a neek. They ignored me. So I queued for a ticket.

Then I saw a team of security people, standing by the barriers, checking hand luggage, sweeping people with hand-held explosives-detectors, like they do at airports and at the London Eye. Some people were made to empty their bags and pockets. What made me stare was what was written on the T-shirts. Kat and I had got it right.

FRONTLINE
SECURITY

It was the same T-shirt as the one worn by the strange man, only this time I could see the missing letters. I scoured the faces of the guards at the entrance, but the strange man wasn't among them. I bought a ticket and presented it. One of the guards waved a bomb-detector around my body and motioned me forward.

As I went through a metal turnstile, the 'person-counter' clicked to a new daily number: 20,054.

I stopped. T is letter 20 in the alphabet, E is letter number 5, and D is letter number 4. It was as if the 'person-counter' had registered me by name: 20, 5, 4. TED. Perhaps it was my lucky day. Perhaps I would find Kat. And perhaps we'd find the strange man. And perhaps this would lead us to Salim. Perhaps—

Perhaps nothing. As I went through into the big hall, I stared. Engines revved, tyres screeched, film tracks blared, lights flashed, music thumped. Everywhere was the smell of petrol and polish. The names of bikes were displayed on every stand. Hondas, Yamahas, Suzukis. One stand said: WELCOME TO BIKER PARADISE. It was more like Biker Hell.

The colours were chrome, black, electric-blue.

The noises were purring engines and throbbing drumbeats.

A giant screen showed motorcycle racers coming straight at you.

Waving girls in black leather bikinis sat on bikes that hung from the air and went nowhere.

I didn't know where to look. People kept thrusting leaflets at me and sticking stickers on my sweatshirt. One woman gave me a raffle ticket. It said: FREE TO ENTER. WIN A SET OF LADY'S LEATHERETTES.

Whatever they were, I didn't want them. I wanted Kat.

I walked among the loud stands. A man approached me with studded gloves and tattoos up his neck. He started talking to me as if he'd known me all my life. He used a lot of words I didn't know. GSX. Disc brakes. Harley's V-Rod. VFR. Kawasaki. He paused.

'Maybe you're the Tornado type?' he said. He put a hand on my arm and pointed to a model overhead with a silver picture on it of a swirling twister, just about to touch down.

'Hrumm,' I said, my hand flapping.

'You're right. It's the best,' he said. 'The *crème de la crème* of motorbikes, the one and only, the . . .'

I ran.

Then an announcement came over the loud speaker. '*Come to the take-off ramp in Hall Two for the freestyle jumper display. Hurry – the show starts in two minutes.'*

There was a general movement in one direction. I found myself being carried along into another big hall. In the centre was a huge ramp. It looked like you would have needed mountaineering equipment to climb it. It stopped in mid-air like a road to nowhere. A terrific drone of an internal combustion engine started up. It turned over with a *wreurrrrrring* noise, becoming ever higher pitched. Then I saw it: a flash of chrome, a white helmet, a missile-like soar. A bike about to jump. It parted company with the top of the ramp. It continued its flight up. It almost grazed the roof. Then down it came, down and down.

I had to shut my eyes because whoever was on it was sure to be smashed up and dead and I didn't want to see it.

The crowd clapped and cheered. I opened my eyes. The bike had landed metres away. There was a bad feeling in my oesophagus. My hands were over my ears. The driver was a madman. He pulled up, got off his bike and took off his helmet.

Long blonde locks fell out. It was a woman, not a man. *Male or female, depending on how you look at it.* The audience gasped. Then there was more clapping, cheers, people thumping their feet. The woman laughed, shook out her hair and waved a leathered hand in the air. She remounted her bike and zoomed back to the start.

Another drone started, another competitor, another zoom, another crazy jump, freestyle, then another.

On the last jump a miracle happened. I saw Kat. She was only a few metres away from me, up front by the railing, staring up at the jumpers. Her eyes and mouth were wide and round like three flying saucers.

I went up to her and pulled the sleeve of her fur-collared jacket. She didn't notice at first. I pulled it again. She spun round. Her eyes opened wider, then scrunched up, and her face folded up small and mean and she bellowed so loud in my ear it hurt.

'Bloody hell, Ted! What are *you* doing here?'

TWENTY-EIGHT

Meetings

'Kat,' I said. My head went off to one side. Even though Kat's voice was like a supersonic boom splitting my eardrum, I was glad. Mr Shepherd says to remember to smile when you greet people, so I smiled. 'Kat.'

Kat looked all around. Her voice dropped to a hiss. 'Are you on your own?'

'Yes.'

'Auntie Glo – Mum – they're not with you?'

'No.'

'They're at home still?'

'Yes.'

'You didn't give me away?'

'No.'

She hugged me. 'Go, bro. So where do they think we are?'

My hand flapped. I stopped it by holding it down with my other hand. 'Not at Tiffany's, Kat,' I said. 'They think we've gone swimming.'

Kat looked at me, her head wagging like one of those toys that sit in the backs of cars. 'Another lie, Ted. One of these days you'll be nearly normal.'

I told her about finding my way on the tube. How I'd cracked the missing letters. How I'd phoned Frontline Security and spoken to the temp.

'I met her,' Kat said. 'I went round there in person. Her name's Claudette. She smokes Charisma cigarettes.'

'She mentioned you,' I said. 'She said you'd been looking for the same man. And Kat . . .'

'What?'

'That was a good lie you told.'

'Which one?'

'The one about the asthma inhaler.'

'Yeah. I was proud of that. It worked, too. She told me his name, Christy, and where he was. Then she told me all about her love life. She said she was bored as hell. She filed her nails, chewed gum and smoked, all at once. And guess what else?'

'What?'

'She offered me a fag.'

'Hrumm.'

'I took it, too.'

'Hrumm.'

'Don't *hrumm* me, Ted. I didn't smoke it. Not really. I had a puff or two. But it wasn't my brand. It tasted like cowshed.'

We walked around the first hall together. Kat didn't seem to mind me being there. Her eyes darted everywhere. She whispered, 'Oh, what I'd do to have one of my own!' She starting picking up the biker language. '*Honda's VFR . . . Buell's Firebolt . . . Guzzi,*' she muttered, dragging me around the stands. I could hardly keep up. She pointed at the metallic paintwork, admiring the biggest, fastest models. She was in Biker Paradise. I was in Biker Hell. Why, I wondered, couldn't we have tracked the strange man to somewhere more tranquil? A flower or antiques show, maybe? Or somewhere really interesting, like the Science Museum?

Then we saw him.

Him. He was standing six metres away, in the same clothes he'd worn on the day at the London Eye, minus the jacket, talking into a two-way radio. Kat dragged me behind a stand. I tugged away from her.

'Don't let him see you,' she hissed.

'Why not?'

'I'm handling this one myself.'

'But—'

'No buts.'

'I'm coming too, Kat.'

'No. You're not. That's an order.'

'An order?'

'Yeah. I can give them. Because I'm older.'

'I'm wiser. You said.'

'Rubbish.'

'You did, Kat. You said you needed my brains.'

Kat's nostrils quivered. She does that when she's about to erupt like a super-volcano. Then she forgot and gripped me instead. 'He's walking this way,' she whispered.

He was right in front of us.

Kat stepped forward. 'Excuse me, sir!' she called.

The man was talking into his radio. He turned

round, saw Kat, put up a hand and went on talking.

We waited.

'Over and out,' he said, into the radio. He stared straight at Kat. 'What can I do for you, young lady?' he said. 'Are you lost?'

Then he smiled. It was a smile I didn't like. One eyebrow went up, his head tilted, he looked Kat up and down. Then he noticed me. My hand flapped up and my head was off to the side. His eyes opened wide and his mouth parted slightly, then he looked over his shoulder and shifted from one foot to the other. A second later his face changed back to a smile, a nanosecond flicker.

'You lost?' he repeated.

Kat smiled back. 'No,' she said.

'On you go, then. Have fun.'

'We're not lost,' Kat explained. 'But we know somebody who is.'

'Oh?'

'We thought you might be able to help.'

'If you've lost somebody, go to the information desk. They'll make an announcement.'

'He didn't get lost here. He got lost two days ago. At the London Eye.'

The man shrugged. 'So?'

'I mean *really* lost. The police are looking for him. It was just after you came up to us and gave us that ticket. Remember?'

The man stared at us for a long time. I looked at his eyes. They narrowed slightly. The pupils seemed to get smaller.

'The Eye . . .' he said. 'So that's where I've seen you before. I never forget a face.'

'You remember?'

'Now I do. I'm frightened of heights, you see. I get terrible vertigo. You're the kids I gave the ticket to, aren't you? But I don't know anything about your lost friend. Fancy our meeting up again. Coincidence, huh?'

I was about to tell him about the letters on his T-shirt, but Kat elbowed me, which means 'Shut up'.

'Yeah. Coincidence,' she said.

'D'you like motorbikes?'

'Yeah,' Kat said. 'They're great.'

'It's a fantastic show this year. Best ever. Did you see the freestyle jumps?'

'Yeah.'

'Did you like them?'

'They were awesome.'

'If I were you, I'd go back to Hall Two. They're giving lessons on the lighter scooters in a minute or two.'

'Really?'

'You'll be zooming around the cones in no time at all.'

'Honest?'

'Sure thing. Off you go. Talk to my mate John in there. He'll get you on a bike first if you mention me.'

'Hey – thanks.'

'Don't mention it. I hope you find your friend.' He saluted us with his radio, smiled and walked off.

'Hrumm,' I said.

Kat's head went off to one side. Her face fell. 'Hell,' she said.

We stood together, jostled by passers-by, and

watched the strange man disappear into the crowd,
just as he'd done at the London Eye.

'Dead end,' Kat said. 'I might have guessed.'

'Guessed what?' I asked.

'It was the road to nowhere.'

'The road to nowhere,' I repeated.

'Stop repeating everything I say! Let's check out
those scooter lessons.'

She dragged me back to the second hall and found
the man called John. I watched as she mounted a
scooter, helmeted. She rode away. She wobbled,
swerved, revved and giggled. My hand flapped up
every time she turned because it looked like she was
going to come off and break her neck. She wound
around the cones and gathered speed. I watched. I
shut my eyes and put my hand in my jacket pocket.
Then I thought.

Salim vanishing. The police searching.

Aunt Gloria wailing. Mum raging.

Kat crying. Me lying.

The strange man . . . His face and eyes when he
first saw us . . . The girl who did the first jump . . .

Vertigo and claustrophobia . . . My brain *wrreeurred* like the bikes.

I opened my eyes.

Kat got off the scooter. She gave back the helmet. She came up to me, smiling with wide open eyes.

'Ted, that was great. You should try it.'

I shook my head. I quoted the graffiti I'd seen on the tube. 'No way.'

'I've been on that bike and I've been round those cones, Ted. And d'you know what?'

'What?'

'When I'm on the bike, that's when I can think.'

'Think?'

'Yeah. I was on the bike and I couldn't hear the noise. The voices faded. I was on my own. Really on my own. All I could hear were my thoughts. My thoughts about Salim. That's when I knew it, Ted.'

'Knew what?'

'Knew he was lying. That man, Christy. He was lying.'

I nodded. I had reached the same conclusion via a process of deductive thought. Our minds had met, which is a way to say that we were thinking the same thing at the same time, which was a rare thing between Kat and me. 'Yes, Kat. He was lying.'

Maybe it was because I'd become a liar myself that day. They say it takes one to know one. I'd known almost as soon as he left us that he'd lied. It wasn't so much what he'd said as how he'd tried to distract us from what we wanted to know. He was a mini Coriolis force, trying to deflect us. There'd been another thing, a contradiction. At the London Eye he'd said he'd decided against the ride because he was frightened of closed-in spaces: claustrophobia. Today he'd said he was frightened of heights: vertigo.

'We've got to find him again,' Kat said, 'and make him tell us the truth.'

'Yes, Kat. The truth.'

'We're a team, you and I. Let's go, Ted.'

TWENTY-NINE

Pursuit

But we couldn't find him.

The exhibition hall was full to bursting. My hand flapped so much that Kat told me to shove it in under my jacket. By now she was reverting to mean, mad Miss Katastrophe and our minds were at polar extremes. We ended up back at the entrance. There were several guards on duty, but the strange man wasn't among them. Kat approached a woman guard, who was in the middle of searching somebody's bag.

''Scuse, miss,' Kat said.

The woman looked round, lips turned down. 'What?' she snapped.

'D'you know where Christy is?'

'Christy? What's it to you?'

'He's a friend. I've a message for him.'

'A message?'

'An important message.'

'What about?'

'It's private.'

'Private?' The woman gave the handbag she was searching back to the owner. 'He's just radioed. He says he's got a stomach bug. He's leaving for the day. Which means me and my two mates, here, we're on our own, right? And we've got no time to stand blathering to his friends. Right?'

'Right,' said Kat.

'With him it's always the same. Sick this, dentist that, dead uncle the other. Never rains but it pours.' Her lips went down. She shook her head. 'Ha-ha. Just like his name. If you *do* catch him up on the way to the tube, give him a message from me. I'm sick of him being sick. He needn't bother coming in tomorrow. He's fired.'

'Fired?' I said, thinking of people being burned on the stake in olden days.

'Fired, sacked, given the boot. Take your pick.'

I stared at her and so did Kat.

Then Kat grabbed me by the sleeve. 'Hurry, Ted!' She dodged past the other people exiting, dragging me with her. I trod on three people's feet, but they were big biker men wearing thick black boots and they didn't notice. We were out in the open air, across the lights, and I'd only just time to notice the weather (high strata cloud, fine sunshine) before we were in the tube station, at the ticket barriers, and we glimpsed the strange man walking towards the eastbound platform.

'It's him,' squeaked Kat. 'Hurry!'

I took my ticket out of my pocket. My hand shook itself out so hard I dropped it. Kat screeched. I picked it up. The machine plucked it from my hand and spat it out on top.

'Pick it up, Ted, pick it up.'

I'd forgotten that the barriers don't open until you've retrieved your ticket. I picked it up and went through.

'*Run!*'

I ran after her, head off to the side. I saw her hurl herself onto a waiting train. The doors beeped, about to close. I stepped on and got trapped. It felt like I was being squeezed from three dimensions into two. Kat heaved at the doors and yanked me in.

'*Oaf!*'

She'd turned into a tornado, an unstoppable force.
'He's in the next carriage down, not far from the
door. I can see him,' she said. 'I'll keep my eye on
him. We'll get off when he does.'

It was a rattling old-style tube-train that screeched
and jerked. We held tight to the bar as it took the
sharper bends. Sloane Square. Victoria. Blackfriars.
Tower Hill. Aldgate East. The tube destination said
UPMINSTER. Were we going all the way out there?
After Stepney Green Kat stooped into a crouch, like
a tiger about to spring, and dragged me into a stoop-
ing position too. 'He's getting up,' she hissed.

The train braked. It pulled into Mile End and
halted. There was a pause. Seconds ticked by.
Everybody waited silently. A man opposite tapped
his foot on the floor. With a *swoosh*, the doors
opened. Kat grabbed me and flew off the train,
almost knocking over a gentleman trying to
board.

'*Sorry!*' she muttered, pulling me after her by the
sleeve of my sweatshirt. She ran behind a chocolate
machine.

The strange man was walking briskly down the platform and up a flight of steps.

'*Now!*' said Kat.

We emerged from behind the chocolate machine. 'Don't run,' Kat said. 'Saunter.'

'Saunter,' I said. I'm not good at sauntering, but I did my best. We sauntered down the platform, up the steps, through the ticket barrier, to the street entrance.

Kat spotted him across the street. We crossed too and did some more sauntering behind him. He never looked round. His hands were in his jacket pockets and his head was down as if he was having a long train of thought. He paused at a corner by some traffic lights and outside a pub called the Falcon Arms. We stopped too. After a moment he went inside the pub.

It was a large, grubby building with big bay windows and no curtains. It had a drooping white banner across the entrance saying OPEN ALL DAY. Above it swung a sign showing a picture of a falcon perched on a branch with a mouse in its beak. You could tell from the way the mouse's tail was flying behind that in the picture there was a strong wind, maybe gale-force seven.

'What now, Kat?' I said.

'We wait,' Kat said.

'Wait,' I said.

'As long as it takes.'

'You know what Dad says.'

'What?'

'Pubs are black holes. People go in there and never come out again.'

'He's only joking, Ted.'

We stood on the street corner for five minutes. Kat got restless. The traffic streamed by. Kat said she felt like a sore thumb. Her thumb looked fine to me. I was just about to ask what she meant when she said, 'I'm gonna sneak up to that pub window, Ted. You stay put.'

I watched her sneak forward. She approached the bay window like a double-o agent on a mission to save the world. 'He's propping up the bar,' she hissed over to me. I imagined a bar on wobbly trestles, liable to fall down at any moment.

She took another look inside. 'He's got a long glass of dark brown stuff in front of him and he's hardly touched it,' she reported. 'He's watching TV on a big screen.'

She rejoined me. 'He could be in there for some time. Let's cross and wait by the television shop near that bus stop. We can watch TV while we wait and people will just think we're waiting for the bus.'

We crossed over by the lights and stared at the TV images in the window: people chatting, laughing, shaking their heads – a mid-afternoon game show. We could see but not hear them. We had eighteen different TVs to choose from but they were all tuned to the same channel. The game show ended and the news came on. Eighteen screens of soldiers in a foreign country, walking up dusty streets with heavy guns. Eighteen screens of African children with flies around their large eyes and no clothes on. You could tell they were starving. Eighteen screens of the prime minister giving a speech at a convention, his two hands shaking themselves out over the podium as he spoke, a bit like mine.

Then. Eighteen screens of our living room. Our sofa, times eighteen, Rashid, times eighteen, Aunt Gloria, with her white sweater, her orange lips and pale cheeks, times eighteen. She was talking. The cameras went in close. I could see the word. *Please*. Kat gasped.

'Auntie Glo!' Kat squeaked. 'Our living room! On TV!'

'I forgot to tell you,' I said.

'You forgot to tell me?'

'They called in the press.'

'The *press*?'

'They came in a big van.'

'They came while I was gone?'

'Yes, Kat.'

'And you didn't tell me?'

'No.'

Kat rolled her eyes.

'I didn't have a chance, Kat. Not with all those motorbikes.'

We watched as the eighteen shots of our living room switched to eighteen pictures of Salim – the one of him in his school blazer looking neither happy nor sad – then to a telephone number for contacting the police.

The story ended. The next was about the latest mission to Mars and showed a robotic probe collecting specimens from the planet crust. Kat stared at it without seeing it, chanting, 'Our living room. On TV,' to herself. I was interested in the pictures of the bare landscape, wondering what the Martian weather conditions were like and if life might ever have existed there. Neither of us noticed until it was too late. A firm hand grasped my shoulder. And Kat's. I turned round. So did Kat. We were face to face with the strange man.

He smelled of alcohol. His eyes were slits. His lips were pressed up tight. I knew what that meant. Anger. Extreme.

His grip hardened on my shoulder so it hurt. 'You again,' he hissed.

THIRTY

The Road to Nowhere

Kat said nothing. I said nothing.

His grip relaxed. He took a step back. He wiped his mouth with the back of his hand. 'You followed me, didn't you? You followed me here from the scooter show.'

Kat nodded.

'That missing kid. The one on the news. Is *that* who you're looking for?'

'Yes,' said Kat. 'He's not just some *kid*. He's our cousin, Salim.'

'Why d'you think I had anything to do with it?'

'Because it was right after you gave us that ticket. Salim went up the London Eye. But he never came down again.'

The strange man looked at us with one side of his lip up, the other down, his nose scrunched up, his eyebrows bunched together. 'Crazy kids!' he said. But he wasn't looking at us. He had his eyes raised upwards as if we were floating above him in the air.

'We're not crazy,' Kat said.

He looked down again and gave a strange kind of smile. 'This cousin of yours – he went up the Eye and never came down, you say?'

'Yes.'

'Kids don't just vanish into thin air.'

Kat sighed. 'That's what the police said.'

The man's eyes shifted round from her face to mine.

'It's serious,' Kat said. 'The police are looking for him. And now it's all over the TV.'

'I don't know anything about it. I told you before.'

'Did you really just buy a ticket – and not decide to use it?'

The man looked around and backed away. 'It wasn't exactly like that,' he said. A bus crammed with passengers had pulled up at the nearby stop. A woman with a buggy struggled to get on. The driver stared at her with his lips turned down. The strange man glanced at the bus, then looked at us.

'It was this bird,' he said, his words speeding up. The bus revved up. The wheels of the buggy spun as the woman seesawed it onto the platform. My hand was shaking itself out.

'This bird in the queue. That's who I got the ticket from.'

'A bird?' I said, thinking of crows and pigeons.

'A dark-haired chick. Nobody I knew. I was just passing. She called me over and said how her boyfriend hadn't shown and she didn't want to waste his ticket but she didn't want to lose her boarding slot either. So she asked me to go over and give it to you.'

'Why us?' said Kat.

The man shrugged. 'Dunno. You were kids, right at the back of queue, I guess. She took pity on you.' Suddenly he dashed over to the bus just before the driver shut the doors. 'It's her you need to talk to. Not me. If you can find her.' Then he gave a strange laugh.

'Wait!' screamed Kat. 'Don't go! Wait!' She ran after him, but the cross-looking driver shook his

head at her and shouted, 'Full up!' and shut the
doors in her face.

The strange man raised his palms upwards as well
as his hands and the bus jerked forward and gathered
speed down the high street.

'Hell!' said Kat.

'Hrumm,' I said.

'Shut up!' Kat shouted.

The bus, along with the strange man, disappeared
under a bridge. Kat clenched her fists and banged
them on her thighs like she was a boxer fighting herself. Then she kicked a Coke can on the pavement
into the gutter. 'The road to nowhere,' she said in a
voice so loud that passers-by stared at us. 'One great
big bloody waste of time.' On the word *time*, she
crushed her boot down on the Coke can. 'Road to
bloody nowhere.' The boot stamped up and down.
The Coke can went pancake-flat. 'Nowhere.' She
burst into tears. 'And which way's the bloody tube?
I've bloody well forgotten.'

THIRTY-ONE

Tornado Touchdown Time

Somehow Kat found the way back to the tube. She stomped up the high street with me trying to keep up and my hand flapping and then she asked directions from a man who was painting a railing and he pointed a finger and she stomped on, acting as if I wasn't there, and I kept up after her until we got to the tube.

We travelled the long way home in silence. Then we walked back up the main road and into our street and she still said nothing but she let me walk beside her now and her lips were turned down, which meant she was sad more than angry.

Outside our house she stopped and said, 'We're for it, Ted. Our hair isn't even wet.'

I touched my hair, confused. Then I remembered. We were supposed to have gone swimming.

'Maybe we can just sneak in,' Kat whispered. She got out her key and was about to put it in the lock when the door flew open.

Mum stood in front of us, barring the way. Her hair was messy and her eyes were as wide as volcano craters. She dangled our swimming gear before our eyes: Kat's bikini, two sets of goggles, my trunks. She spluttered, dropped the lot, hugged us, cuffed Kat round the ear and screeched, 'You disobedient, lying, cheeky chit – and as for you, Ted, I'm shocked, I don't know what got into you, writing that lie about going swimming, I've been worried witless, I've—'

Kat walked past her with her hands over her ears.

'Don't you swan off like that until I've finished with you!'

I hovered in the doorway, frowning and thinking of swans gliding away in the pond in the park. Then I mumbled, 'Sorry, Mum, sorry, Mum,' because I knew she was angry, but she didn't hear me. I picked up the things she'd dropped. She yanked me into the house and slammed the door.

'That Mrs Hopper across the road's peering out again. God only knows what the neighbours think! TV crews, police cars, I've just about had it, Gloria's gone mental, you two vanish. Have you any idea how I've been feeling?'

Kat laughed. She kicked the skirting board and hooted. 'The *neighbours*,' she screeched. She doubled over. 'Typical grown-up crap.' Her voice went up an octave and she crooned, '*God only knows what the neighbours think*. Is that all you care about, Mum? What the neighbours think? We've been trying to help. Trying to find Salim. But you're not interested, are you? You don't want to know what we think, do you? All you care about is *what the neighbours think*. Salim might be dead for all you care.'

Mum stood eyeball to eyeball with Kat. I realized they were exactly the same height.

'Don't you dare say that – don't you dare . . .'

Mum's hand darted up as if to hit Kat hard on the cheek, but it froze about a centimetre off target. Her voice trailed off.

The temperature in the hallway seemed to plummet to minus thirty degrees.

Kat stared at Mum, her eyes round. 'Go on, hit me,' she hissed.

Mum shook her head and I could see tears falling down her cheek. Her hand fell to her side.

I stepped forward. 'Mum? Kat?' I said, but they paid no attention.

Then Kat's lips started to wobble. She pushed Mum out of her way, wailing, '*I hate you, I hate you.*' She ran upstairs, tripping halfway. *Hate you, hate you*. A bedroom door slammed. Then something upstairs crashed.

It was Tornado Touchdown Time, or T x 3, in our house. This is my way of describing what it's like when people have really bad arguments and it is the worst place to be in all the world.

Mum slumped on the bottom stair, head down in her hands. Her shoulders heaved and she made a strange noise.

I'd never seen Mum like that before.

'Oh no,' she moaned, rocking herself. 'Is there no end to this?' I wasn't sure whom she was talking to and looked around. I was the only one there. Which meant she was talking either to me or to God. 'Oh God, oh God,' she said.

So it was God, not me, and I was free to go.

I decided to check out the weather in the back garden.

THIRTY-TWO

Solar Wind

I walked fast through the kitchen and out into the back garden, my hand flapping. *The general synopsis at eighteen hundred issued by the Met Office: Fitzroy, mainly northerly, four or five, becoming variable, thundery showers . . .* I did my pacing, counting the strides it took to get from one side of the back garden to the other. Twelve-and-a-half strides long, seven across. I ducked under the line of dry clothes, grabbing onto a sheet. I left a grubby stain. My fingers were still black from going through the phonebook earlier. *Eye of the Needle Solutions*. That's what I needed. A solution for the impossible. How you get through a needle point. How you disappear from a sealed pod. I thought of the girl on the motorbike, the pink sleeve in the photo, I thought of Dad's razor blade, I thought of the strange man and the lady saying how he was fired and him saying we should find the 'bird' with the dark hair, and I thought of what Aunt Gloria had said earlier. 'If brains alone could bring Salim back, yours would do it, Ted.'

I held my hands over my ears and shook out my head. My brain felt like it was overheated, going into melt-down. I paced the garden and recounted my steps, only this time the number came out wrong — eleven-and-a-half strides instead of twelve-and-a-half, so either my legs had grown in the last few minutes, or the universe had shrunk, instead of expanded. 'Wreuurrrrr,' I went, like the Earl's Court motorbikes. I looked up at the sky. Evening. High strata cloud, fresh southwesterly, but air pressure falling. One of Dad's shirts on the line flapped against my head. The wind was picking up. I walked over to the garden shed and kicked it a few times.

I'm not a philosopher. I'm a meteorologist. But I believe in meditation. Buddhists believe that if you empty out your head, that's when you find enlightenment. Kicking the shed is a good way of emptying out your head. It's like jumping on a trampoline. You kick or jump, you jump or kick, and eventually all the thoughts march out of your ears, like a line of toy soldiers heading for the edge of the table. You're left with nothing – the empty nothing I told Salim about, which is frightening and lonely, but simple and clear.

I shut my eyes and imagined a vast, silent void. I kept up the kicking. By the eighty-seventh kick I was empty inside and a kind of solar wind arrived in my brain. A storm of charged particles rushed through my head like lightning, giving off strange flashes of coloured lights. A picture formed. It was like the Aurora Borealis burning in my brain. It sparkled so hard it hurt. The pattern I'd half glimpsed earlier that day flooded back. But this time it didn't vanish. I caught it. I hung onto it. I made it freeze, like ice.

Then I knew. Not where Salim was. But how he'd vanished like he had.

THIRTY-THREE

The Sound of the Storm

When you try to talk to people in the middle of a storm, they can't hear. They can't catch your words for the sound of the storm.

Thunder, rain and wind.

And the things the storm moves – leaves, roof tiles, rubbish.

I came in from the garden, eighty-seven kicks of the garden shed wiser, but I couldn't make myself heard. Dad was just coming in from work. Mum was still sitting on the stairs. She ran to him before he took off his coat. Her arms went around him and she put her head on his shoulder.

'Oh, Ben, I'm so glad you're home.'

'Faith, love – what's wrong? Has there been bad news?'

'Not since we spoke earlier. The press has been here. Twice. Glo's been terrible all day. This afternoon she had a panic attack. She couldn't breathe. I called the doctor. He gave her a sleeping pill. She's upstairs, flat out, the first proper sleep she's had since Salim went missing. Then the kids just took off somewhere without asking. And Ted left a note about going swimming. Imagine! He *lied*, Ben. I didn't know what to do. I thought we'd lost them too. Then Rashid went out to walk the streets. He said he was going mad sitting around, waiting. And just now the kids came back. Oh Ben, the relief. They came in the door, and Kat and I – Kat and I—'

'Shush . . .'

'We had a row.'

'So what's new?'

'A terrible row, Ben. I nearly hit her, I came this close . . .' She held out her finger and thumb, a centimetre apart. Then she started wailing again. Dad said 'Shush' but she didn't stop. I stood a couple of metres away.

'Dad,' I said. He didn't answer.

'Mum,' I said. She didn't answer.

I waited and tried again. 'Dad. Mum.'

Mum looked round and swallowed. She said, 'Oh,

Ted. There you are. Can't you go upstairs and read a book or something?'

'But Mum, I've worked out—'

'Shush, Ted,' Dad said. 'Now isn't the time.'

The words were hard and short, not like Dad's voice at all, and Mum started crying again, so I went upstairs.

In my room Kat lay face down on the lilo, her fist clenched up and pressed between her eyebrows. I noticed that my alarm clock was on the floor, broken into bits. That was the smashing sound I'd heard earlier at Tornado Touchdown Time.

'Kat,' I said.

She shook her head. Her eyes scrunched up. A tear slipped out and trailed down her nose. She didn't wipe it away.

'Kat. I think I've got it.'

She moaned.

'The theories. The nine theories. I think I know the right one.'

'Oh, Ted! You and your theories.' She grabbed a pillow and buried her head under it.

I went up to her and tapped her shoulder. 'The theories, Kat,' I said.

She looked up from the pillow. 'Go away,' she said.

'Kat,' I said. Then I added, 'Sis,' because she likes me calling her this as she says it makes me sound normal. But this time it didn't work.

'Ted – I don't want to know. Go to hell.'

'Kat . . .'

She took the pillow and banged me on the shoulder with it. 'That's to stop you looking like a bloody duck that's forgotten how to quack,' she said. Then she threw herself down and sobbed.

Next I crept into Kat's room, where Aunt Gloria was. 'Aunt Gloria?' I whispered.

But Aunt Gloria was fast asleep. This was not surprising as Mum had said she'd had a sleeping pill. Sleeping pills make your brain waves calm down into a sleep pattern. (I would like to try one, not so much because I have trouble sleeping, but more to see if my brain with its different operating system would respond.) Aunt Gloria lay on her back diagonally across the bed, her foot hanging over the edge and the duvet crooked. Her mouth was half open, her breathing loud and low. Her eyelids were a bruised colour, a purple smudge. I couldn't have woken her even if I'd tried.

I was about to creep out again when I saw Kat's copy of *The Tempest*, face down on the duvet. Kat, like Salim, had been studying it at school. Had Aunt Gloria been reading it too? Salim had said he'd acted in it and that it was right up my street. I realized now that he'd meant that I would like it, because it was named after a dramatic weather condition and weather is what interests me most. I picked it up, sat down at Kat's desk and began to read.

First there was a long list of people. This is how plays always start. The author tells you who is who and how they are related to each other and it is called a cast of characters. This one had a lot of men and some strange-sounding spirits and a female called Miranda, who I remembered Kat saying was a dishrag. Then I read the first scene. I didn't understand it because the language was almost as hard to understand as French, which is my worst subject at school. I read it again, and a third time, before I worked out that it was about a ship sinking in a storm. That was as far as I got when a groan behind me made me look up.

'Salim?' It sounded as if Aunt Gloria was speaking in her sleep. 'Salim?'

I crept over to the side of the bed, *The Tempest* open in my hand. 'No, Aunt Gloria,' I said. 'It's Ted.'

She looked at me. The whites of her eyes were bloodshot, which is what happens when you have been crying or staring too hard for too long at something.

'Ted?' she said. She saw the copy of *The Tempest* and smiled. 'I was reading that just now, to help me sleep. Salim was in it last term.'

'I know, Aunt Gloria. He told me.'

She smiled. 'The dashing young prince. Ferdinand. My Salim.'

She turned onto her side and curled up, crying. I stood there in silence, not sure if I should put my hand on her shoulder or do nothing. After a while I realized she had gone back to sleep. I put the play back down by her side and left the room.

Out on the landing I stood and listened to the house. It was quiet. I wondered why nobody could hear me when it was so quiet. Then I started to hear the sounds houses always make when the people in them are silent. Boards creaking as they settle onto the foundations. Pipes gurgling inside the walls. Central heating humming. I clung to the banister at the top of the stairs. I heard something else: my heart thumping, blood pumping in my ears, the distant tick of the clock in the hallway downstairs. It was time. Time had a sound too. I'd never heard it before. I put my hands over my ears. It was deafening.

Mum appeared at the bottom of the stairs. She came up silently and gave me a hug. I squirmed.

'Ted,' she said, 'I apologize. To you. But especially to Kat.'

'Mum . . .' I said. 'I've worked it out.'

She patted my head as if I'd said nothing, went past me and knocked on my bedroom door. There was no reply, but she turned the handle and went in. She shut the door behind her. I heard her voice, soft and sad, coming from the other side. Then I heard Kat's. I couldn't hear their words.

I went on downstairs just as Rashid let himself in through the front door with the spare key. He stood in the hallway, looking ahead with no expression on his face that I could decipher.

'Uncle Rashid . . .' I said.

'Sorry?' he said. 'Oh. Hello, Ted.'

Dad came out of the living room and greeted him by saying, 'Do you want a can of beer?' and they went into the kitchen.

Just as if I didn't exist.

Then I went into the front room. I went over to the mantelpiece and picked up Detective Inspector Pearce's card. I stared at it. I'm no good at telephone conversations. But I remembered how she'd smiled at me when I told her about Salim getting a call on his mobile and said how she wished her officers had half my brains. She'd listened then.

I normally only use the telephone about once a

week. This is because I have nobody I need to telephone but sometimes Mum makes me call the Directory Enquiries number as she says I need the practice. Today, I was about to use the telephone twice, which was far more practice than I wanted. I sat on the side of the sofa, on top of my flapping hand. I picked up the phone with my other hand. Then I dialled Detective Inspector Pearce's number.

THIRTY-FOUR

Smoke

Time passed.

Kat and Mum came downstairs arm in arm. I hadn't seen them like that in a while. I was able to deduce from their body language that they had made up and this made me pleased because it showed how much better I was getting at reading body language.

Then Aunt Gloria came down in her dressing gown. Her lips were flat and her eyes empty-looking, so I didn't know what her body language was saying and I was less pleased.

Dad and Rashid went out to fetch an Indian take-away for everyone. They returned with a dozen foil containers of steaming food. I had two samosas, a chicken biryani and most of Kat's chicken korma, which she couldn't finish. Dad got most of the way through a prawn bhuna. As for the others, mounds of food got left on their plates. Aunt Gloria nibbled on one side of an onion bhajee for about half an hour. Mum's fork went round her plate, pushing the same chickpea. Rashid sipped a beer and stared at his food without even starting.

'How was work?' Mum said to Dad.

He shrugged. 'Quiet. I was out Peckham way today. On another job.'

Then nobody spoke.

I wanted to tell them what I knew and all about my conversation with Detective Inspector Pearce but she had told me to say nothing for now in case people started to hope. She explained that normally hope is a good thing, but if you hope a lot for something and it doesn't happen, then you are disappointed and it's called being let down. I asked her if 'being let down' was like coming back to earth with a bump if you let air out of a hot-air balloon too fast, and she said yes, it was like that.

Then that started another train of thought – that hot-air ballooning was something I'd try one day, but only when the weather was set fair, and I'd bring instruments for measuring air pressure and temperature and make recordings and—

'Houston calling Planet Pluto,' Dad said.

I looked over at Dad. This is what he says to get my attention when my thoughts are far away from where my body is.

'Pass the rice, Ted,' he said, smiling.

I passed the rice. There was silence again.

It was as if everybody had decided that Salim was not to be mentioned. Kat kept winding a brown curl of hair around her finger. Aunt Gloria lit a cigarette but forgot to smoke it. I watched it burn away, and followed the trail of smoke through the air as it burned. It was deflected to the left over her shoulder, although there was no window open and no air in the room. This made me think of the Coriolis effect again and how it is invisible but can make things change direction.

'Aunt Gloria—' I said.

'Shush, Ted,' Mum said.

'No – let him say what he wanted to say,' said Aunt Gloria.

'Why are you lighting cigarettes and not smoking them?' I asked.

'Ted!' said Mum. 'Give your Auntie Glo a break.'

Aunt Gloria gave a tiny smile. 'I didn't even notice I'd lit one, Ted. I tell you what. When this is over – if Salim – if he comes back safe, I'll give the damn things up. That's a promise.'

She sat back, tears going down her face, and took a long drag. I wasn't sure if she was crying at the thought of having to give up cigarettes or because Salim might not come back safely. The room went quiet again. 'If he comes back safe,' she repeated. Which was how I knew she was crying because of Salim, not the cigarettes.

I carried on eating. When I put my knife and fork down, I listened to the silence. I heard the clock ticking again. Then I felt blood pounding in my ears. It was like railway wheels going round in my head, trains of thought running out of control, couplers snapping. *The boy on the slab, the boy on the train.* Mum made a pot of tea. I heard a spoon rapping against china as Dad stirred in his sugar. *Salim or not Salim.*

'I can't stand it any more,' Aunt Gloria said. She leaped up. 'The waiting. I can't stand it.'

Mum reached out and put a hand on Aunt Gloria's wrist. 'I know, Glo. Sit down.'

'You don't know. You can't know. Kat and Ted, they've never disappeared. Not like this. Not for more than two days. And nothing. No news. Nothing.'

'Calm down, Gloria,' said Rashid.

'How can I? You're all sitting there. You're all looking at me. And I know what you're thinking.'

'Glo—' Mum said.

'Don't you start – I overheard you today on the phone to Ben. You think Salim's run away, don't you? You think he's hiding – hiding from me, don't you? Why don't you just say it?'

'Glo—' Mum said.

'Go on – say it.'

'Maybe – if the choice is between Salim being kidnapped by some evil person – or his hiding somewhere, unaware of how much distress he's causing you – then, yes, I do think – that is, I—'

'You're saying it's my fault. That I've brought this on myself.'

'No, Glo, not that, but maybe going to New York, for Salim, that was a step too—'

'It wasn't, it wasn't,' Aunt Gloria cried out. 'I know my own boy. He wouldn't do this to me, I know . . .'

She turned from the table. The sleeve of her dressing gown caught her plate and an onion bhajee went flying. Her shoulders shook. 'I'm going to go out there and find him. I am. I don't care if I have to walk from one end of London to the other.' She staggered through the door into the hallway.

Mum jumped up. 'Glo! Don't go! I didn't mean . . .'

From where I was sitting I could see Aunt Gloria opening the front door, fiddling with the handle. 'Get lost, Fai,' she shouted.

'Stop her, Ben,' Mum said. 'She's out of her mind.'

Dad, looking dazed, got to his feet. Kat got up too. Rashid sat still, his mouth hanging open.

Just as Aunt Gloria opened the front door, a siren came wailing up right outside. Lights flashed. There were voices in the front garden, people moving, confusion. A chair fell over and Rashid rocked on his chair and started groaning. 'Please God, please, no,' he said.

A bad feeling went up my oesophagus.

The police had come, just when Detective Inspector Pearce had told me they would.

But I hadn't expected the siren.

And it didn't sound like the sirens did when I'd played ambulances with Kat.

It sounded real and near and loud and bad.

The boy on the train. The boy on the slab. Salim or not Salim. I put my hands over my ears. *The general synopsis at nineteen hundred: low Fitzroy a thousand and eight expected just west of Rockall . . .*

THIRTY-FIVE

The Boy on the Train Again

Detective Inspector Pearce entered the house, leading Aunt Gloria by the elbow. She guided her into the kitchen and sat her down.

'She looks like she needs a warm drink,' the inspector said. 'She's in a state of shock.' Kat poured a cup of tea. Rashid got up to give his place to Aunt Gloria. He sat her down and stroked her hair. Her hands shook and her lips chattered together as if she'd just come in from a snowstorm although it was warm and humid outside, about eighteen degrees.

'Is there news?' Mum said.

Detective Inspector Pearce didn't reply until Aunt Gloria had taken a sip of her drink.

I felt Kat's hand in mine, gripping hard.

Inspector Pearce shook her head. 'Some news, but neither good, nor bad. It's more an update. Courtesy of Ted.'

Everybody stared at me.

'Ted?' said Mum.

'Ted?' said Dad.

'Ted?' said Kat.

I didn't say anything. I looked at the kitchen floor.

'Ted has worked out what happened to Salim the day he disappeared,' Detective Inspector Pearce continued. 'His conclusions agreed with where our enquiries were heading, but I have to say he got there before us.'

'Ted!' Kat said again. Her mouth was open and her jaw hung down.

'We followed up on what Ted told us, but as yet we still don't know where Salim is.'

Aunt Gloria moaned and put her head in her hands.

'But we know who the boy on the train was.'

'Salim?' said Mum.

Detective Inspector Pearce's hands went apart. 'Not Salim,' she said. 'This is the boy on the train, here.'

Another woman police officer, in uniform, came into the room. With her was a boy, about Salim's age, but not Salim. He was half hiding behind the officer's tall body. He was chubby around the cheeks, dark-haired and Asian-looking, although it was hard to see him properly as he wore the hood of his sweat-shirt over his head and part of his face.

'*You!*' Aunt Gloria gasped.

'Hello, Marcus,' I said.

THIRTY-SIX

Weather Detection

I suppose you want to know how I worked it out. Or maybe your brain works on a different operating system from other people's like mine and you've worked it out too.

I'd done nothing but think from two minutes past noon on the day Salim disappeared, Monday, to when I'd phoned the police at 18.04, Wednesday. That's fifty-four hours and two minutes of thinking, if you count sleeping time, which I do. You go on thinking in your sleep.

I'd gone over the nine theories again and again. We'd discounted theories one, two and eight by checking them out. Salim couldn't have stayed on the pod for another ride, nor had my watch gone wrong, nor could he have hidden under somebody's clothes without our noticing. Kat had convinced me that theory nine, that Salim had never got on the pod in the first place, was wrong. Theories five and seven (spontaneous combustion and the time warp)

Kat had dismissed out of hand. I hadn't. But there was another reason I'd finally agreed to cross them off, one I hadn't told Kat. I'd counted the number of people who'd got on the pod. Twenty-one. And I counted the number who'd got off. Twenty-one. I realized that if Salim had spontaneously combusted or slipped into a time warp, only *twenty* people would have got off.

That left theories three, four and six. Three and four both depended on us having somehow missed Salim when he got out. I'd told the police there was only about a 2 per cent chance of our having missed him. Which meant there was a 98 per cent chance that Salim had emerged from the pod in disguise.

At first we'd thought this theory unlikely. But the more I considered it over the fifty-four hours and two minutes, the more possible it seemed. When we went up in the London Eye with Dad the next day, I'd noticed a time when you could put a disguise on with nobody noticing. It's when everyone turns to have their souvenir shot taken. Everyone faces one way for almost a full minute until the flash goes off.

So I'd given the souvenir shot of Salim's pod that Kat bought another look. I kept coming back to the pink sleeve – the one that we thought was the girl in the pink fluffy jacket at the back of the picture, waving at the camera. I don't know when I first realized. Maybe it was the eighteen pictures that Kat took of our washing line when she was using up Salim's film, with the sleeves of sweatshirts, jumpers and blouses waving in the wind. Or maybe it was the way I'd seen Kat struggle into her fur-collared jacket, the morning she'd rushed out to get the photos of the strange man enlarged. The sleeve in the souvenir shot was not somebody waving. It was somebody changing.

A pink sleeve. Waving or drowning. Waving or changing. It depended on how you looked at it.

The girl in the pink fluffy jacket was Salim's accomplice. They'd swapped identities in the pod. A wig, a jacket, sunglasses. That was all it needed.

And I remembered Aunt Gloria saying how Salim was a practical joker. Not a theoretical joker, like me, but a practical one, which means he actually carried out his jokes. Maybe this was a practical joke on a big scale.

For a brief period I wondered if Salim had a girl-friend. A girlfriend whom nobody had mentioned. Maybe a girlfriend even Aunt Gloria didn't know about. A factor X in the equation. The Coriolis force. The thing that had deflected Salim off his course. Then, in the fifty-four hours and two minutes of thinking time, another possibility occurred to me.

Marcus. The 'Paki-Boy'. The 'mosher'. The boy in *The Tempest*.

Salim said a 'mate' had called him *from Manchester* while we were crossing the Jubilee footbridge on the way to the Eye. Later we'd heard from the police that everybody questioned in Manchester, including Marcus, had said they'd not heard from Salim since he'd left. It was an inconsistency. Someone was lying.

Marcus, maybe.

The police reported on Salim's friends' alibis the day he disappeared. Marcus's mum had said he was on a day out with the scouts. So I thought, maybe Marcus was out with the scouts the way Kat and I had gone swimming, or the way Kat was supposed to be at school that day when really she'd gone up to town to have her Hair Flair consultation. I didn't know much about Marcus. Only that he and Salim were friends. That they were both half Asian, at an all-boys school. That they were moshers, which means casual, cool dudes. That they'd starred in *The Tempest* at school. Salim had played Ferdinand. Somebody must have played the only female role – Miranda, who Kat had told me was a dishrag. Maybe it was Marcus. Maybe that's how they'd had the idea.

Marcus. Very likely.

When the girl had got off the motorbike at the scooter show freestyle jumps, everybody had assumed she was a man, until she'd taken off her helmet and loosed her long hair. Maybe Kat and I had done the reverse: assumed the person in the pink fluffy jacket was a woman, just because she had long hair. Male or female, it depended how you looked at it.

Marcus. Almost certainly.

Of the twenty-one people leaving the pod, there had been no extra woman, no female who could have emerged from under the wig and sunglasses disguise. But there had been a lad. The lad we'd taken for the girl in the pink fluffy jacket's boyfriend. The boy with chubby, brownish cheeks.

Marcus. Definitely.

That's when I remembered Salim shaving off his moustache. If he was to become the girl in the pink fluffy jacket, he needed to be clean-shaven. As did Marcus. Everything pointed to Marcus. Then the final jigsaw piece fell into place: what the woman security guard said as we left Earl's Court. I didn't slot it into the rest of the pattern until the eighty-seventh kick of the garden shed. Kat had asked her where the strange man called Christy had gone. She'd replied he'd gone home with a stomach bug. A bug she didn't believe in. *With him it's always the same . . . Sick this, dentist that, dead uncle the other. Never rains but it pours . . . Just like his name.*

Detective Inspector Pearce had mentioned

Marcus's surname to us only once, but once was enough. Enough for me, at least, because I am going to be a meteorologist when I grow up. The name Flood had struck me as interesting all along. The strange man had lied to us in Earl's Court and lied to us again in Mile End. Both times he'd known more than he said. He and Marcus were related. They were both called Flood. For some reason he had helped Marcus and Salim carry out their practical joke, maybe because that's all he thought it was. But it wasn't just a practical joke. It was also part of a bigger plan. A plan for Salim to run away.

Because I think everybody knew by then. Salim hadn't been abducted. He'd vanished by his own choice. He'd never wanted to go to New York. A clue to this had been the guidebook in his backpack. There were no creases on the spine, which meant Salim had never opened it. Which meant going to New York didn't make him excited. But the London Eye did. And vanishing while riding it was the best and most exciting way of running away he could think of.

A weather detective is somebody who uses observations and measurements to make theories, and if the theories are right, they will correctly predict weather patterns. Finding out what had happened to Salim and where he was likely to be was exactly like that. I made observations and constructed theories and then found out more facts with Kat's help, and when the facts and the theories fitted, I thought we'd be able to track Salim down, just like you track a storm system and predict where it will make landfall.

Only something had gone wrong.

Salim hadn't appeared at the end of the trail.

There was only Marcus.

And Marcus stood in the kitchen staring at the floor, and when everybody started talking at once to him, he started crying. His head was down but you could hear him and see his shoulders moving.

And I got a very bad feeling in my oesophagus again.

THIRTY-SEVEN

Salim Supreme

Aunt Gloria loomed over Marcus in her dressing gown like a force-ten gale. 'What do you know, Marcus? Where's Salim?' She grabbed Marcus's sleeve. 'Say something! Speak!'

Detective Inspector Pearce led her back to her chair. Mum brought Marcus a drink of lemonade and led him to another chair, but he refused to sit down or take the drink. He shook his head and his hood fell back. Then he wiped his face on his sleeve and looked up and stared at me. I remembered to lift up my lips, which Mr Shepherd says to do when you meet somebody new because it means you can be their friend. But Marcus's lips didn't move, which meant he didn't want to be my friend.

'Marcus is here to say sorry,' Detective Inspector Pearce said. 'He was too frightened to come forward earlier. He thought he'd get into trouble. Now he's told us what he knows. I have here the statement he made earlier. And his story starts out just as Ted worked it out.' She nodded at Kat. 'With Kat's help, I understand.'

'My help?' said Kat.

'I'd never have worked it out without you, Kat,' I said.

Detective Inspector Pearce continued. 'Marcus's mum is outside in a squad car, with another officer, waiting. She wanted you to hear his story too. When he's done, we'll take them home.'

'But I don't understand . . .' Rashid squeezed his knuckles into his head.

'Marcus and Salim spent several hours together the day Salim disappeared,' Inspector Pearce explained. 'Didn't you, Marcus?'

Marcus nodded.

'By arrangement. Then Marcus went back to Manchester on his own. Salim didn't go. But he was supposed to, wasn't he, Marcus?'

Marcus nodded again.

'You see, Salim had planned to run away.'

'No,' Aunt Gloria moaned, putting her head in her hands.

'But he didn't. Not in the end. He changed his mind.'

Aunt Gloria looked up. 'He changed his mind,' she said softly. She nodded. 'That's right. He changed his mind.'

'Do you want to explain, Marcus?' Detective Inspector Pearce asked. 'Or would you rather I read out your statement?'

There was a pause. Marcus put his hood back up so his face was hidden again. A voice you could hardly hear said, 'The statement, miss.' So Detective Inspector Pearce read out Marcus's statement and this is what it said.

POLICE TRANSCRIPT OF STATEMENT MADE BY WITNESS MARCUS FLOOD

MY NAME IS MARCUS FLOOD AND THIS IS THE TRUTH. SALIM IS MY BEST MATE BECAUSE BEFORE HE JOINED MY SCHOOL LAST SEPTEMBER THEY CALLED ME PAKI-BOY BUT NOW THEY DON'T. I'M NOT FROM PAKISTAN. MY MAM'S FROM BANGLADESH AND MY DAD'S IRISH

BUT THAT DIDN'T STOP JASON SMART GRABBING MY SANDWICHES EVERY DAY AND SAYING WHAT'S THE CURRIED GOAT LIKE TODAY, PAKI-BOY, AND THROWING THEM ON THE FLOOR EVEN THOUGH THEY WERE JUST CHEESE AND TOMATO.

THEN SALIM JOINED MY CLASS AND SAT NEXT TO ME. THEY CALLED HIM PAKI-BOY NUMBER TWO BUT HE DIDN'T TAKE ANY NOTICE, EVEN WHEN JASON SMART GRABBED HIS SANDWICHES AND THREW THEM ON THE FLOOR SAYING THEY SMELLED WORSE THAN A YAK'S BUM. THE NEXT DAY JASON SMART OPENED HIS OWN SANDWICH BOX AND THERE WERE THOUSANDS OF MAG-GOTS HEAVING IN IT. THE WHOLE CLASS WAS IN FITS. SALIM WENT FROM PAKI-BOY NUMBER TWO TO MOSHER-SALIM-SUPREME AND SINCE I WAS HIS FRIEND, WE WERE MOSHERS TOGETHER. WE HAD OUR SHIRTS HALF TUCKED IN, HALF OUT, THE TOP MOSHERS OF 9K.

WHEN YOU'RE A MOSHER YOU'RE NOT SUPPOSED TO BE KEEN. YOU SIT AT THE BACK OF THE CLASS AND LOOK DEAD BORED. BUT WITH DRAMA IT WAS DIFFER-ENT. WE WERE THE MOSHER KEENERS BECAUSE MR DAVISON WAS SO COOL. HE CHOSE US TO STAR IN THE

SCHOOL PLAY AT EASTER, THE TEMPEST. MR DAVISON PLAYED PROSPERO, SALIM WAS FERDINAND AND I WAS MIRANDA. HA-HA. THE GIRL. MY VOICE HADN'T BROKEN THEN. I'D A LONG DARK WIG TO WEAR AND A WHITE DRESS AND EVERY TIME I SAID I WAS 'CERTAINLY A MAID', THE WHOLE CLASS CHEERED AND STAMPED THEIR FEET AND I'D ROLL MY EYES AND EVERYBODY WENT 'OOH-LA-LA'. MR DAVISON SAID I WAS A COMIC GENIUS.

THEN, AFTER EASTER, SALIM CAME BACK TO SCHOOL WITH BAD NEWS. HIS MUM WAS MOVING TO NEW YORK AND TAKING HIM WITH HER. I WAS GUTTED. I SAT IN SCIENCE AND TECHNOLOGY, THINKING HOW I'D PINCH SOME CHEMICALS AND SWALLOW THEM WHOLE BECAUSE I COULDN'T STAND THE THOUGHT OF GOING BACK TO BEING PAKI-BOY. WITHOUT SALIM, THAT'S WHAT I'D BE.

SALIM DIDN'T WANT TO GO EITHER. HE ASKED HIS DAD IF HE COULD GO AND LIVE WITH HIM, BUT HIS DAD SAID NO. THEN HIS MUM BOOKED THE TICKETS. THEY WERE TO FLY OUT FROM LONDON SO THAT SHE AND SALIM COULD VISIT THESE RELATIONS THEY HADN'T

SEEN IN YEARS CALLED THE SPARKS. SALIM SAID THE SPARKS COULD BURN IN HELL. I SAID AT LEAST HE'D GET TO FLY THE LONDON EYE, WHICH WAS SOMETHING WE'D ALWAYS DREAMED OF DOING TOGETHER. BUT SALIM SAID FLYING IT WITHOUT ME WOULDN'T BE ANY FUN. THAT'S WHEN WE HAD THE BIG IDEA.

WE'D MEET UP, ME IN MY MIRANDA DISGUISE, AND RIDE THE LONDON EYE TOGETHER. THEN HE'D TAKE THE DISGUISE AND VANISH AND TOGETHER WE'D RUN OFF, LEAVING HIS MUM AND THE SPARKS BEHIND. WE'D GET A TRAIN BACK TO MANCHESTER TOGETHER LATER THAT DAY AND HE'D HIDE OUT SOMEWHERE AND I'D BRING HIM FOOD, AND WHEN HIS MUM'S FLIGHT HAD TAKEN OFF TO NEW YORK WITHOUT HIM, HE'D GO AND LIVE WITH HIS DAD AND HIS DAD WOULD HAVE NO CHOICE BUT TO SAY YES. THEN HE AND I COULD GO ON BEING THE TOP MOSHERS OF 9K.

THE FIRST THING I DID WAS RING CHRISTY, MY BIG BROTHER. CHRISTY'S DOWN IN LONDON AND HE'S ALWAYS CALLING TO ASK FOR MONEY AND DAD TELLS HIM HE'S NOT A BOTTOMLESS PIT AND TO GET LOST. THIS TIME I RANG HIM. I SAID IF HE MET ME AT THE

LONDON EYE AND HELPED ME AND MY MATE SALIM CARRY OUT THIS JOKE WE WERE PLANNING, WE'D GIVE HIM A TENNER. AND HE SAID YES.

SALIM WENT DOWN TO LONDON WITH HIS MUM ON SUNDAY. THE NEXT DAY I TOLD MY MUM I WAS OFF OUT FOR THE DAY WITH THE SCOUTS AND SHE BELIEVED ME AND EVEN GAVE ME SOME MONEY. PLUS SALIM HAD GIVEN ME HIS SAVINGS, SO I HAD MORE THAN ENOUGH TO BUY TWO LONDON EYE TICKETS. THEN I HOPPED ON AN EARLY TRAIN TO LONDON AND DIDN'T PAY A PENNY BECAUSE THERE'S THIS TRICK I KNOW TO DODGE THE TICKET COLLECTORS. I GOT OFF AT EUSTON STATION AND FOUND MY WAY DOWN TO THE RIVER AND THERE WAS THE EYE. YOU COULDN'T MISS IT.

CHRISTY SHOWED UP FIRST. I PUT ON THE WIG I'D WORN AS MIRANDA AND THESE SLICK SUNGLASSES I BOUGHT IN THE COSTA DEL SOL LAST SUMMER, PLUS A JACKET I'D PINCHED FROM SHANNON, MY OLDER SISTER. CHRISTY ROARED HIS HEAD OFF AND SAID I WAS A CRAZY TRANSVESTITE AND DAD WOULD SKIN ME ALIVE IF HE COULD SEE ME. WE BOUGHT TWO TICKETS. I DIDN'T TELL HIM THAT SALIM WAS GOING TO RUN

AWAY AND I WAS GOING TO HIDE HIM. I SAID WE WERE
PLAYING A JOKE ON SALIM'S COUSINS, THE SPARKS.
MY VOICE HAD BROKEN SINCE BEING IN THE PLAY. NO
WAY COULD I GO UP TO THESE SPARK COUSINS MYSELF.
YOU'D HAVE SPOTTED I WASN'T A GIRL THE MOMENT
I OPENED MY MOUTH. THAT'S WHY WE NEEDED
CHRISTY. PLUS HE WAS AN ADULT AND NOBODY WOULD
ASK ANY QUESTIONS WHEN WE BOUGHT THE TICKETS.

WE'D GOT THE TICKETS. I CALLED SALIM TO SEE
WHERE HE WAS. 'HURRY UP,' I SAID. 'WE'RE BOARDING
AT ELEVEN THIRTY.' HE SAID HE WAS JUST COMING
OVER THE RIVER AND MINUTES LATER HE ARRIVED. THE
MUMS WENT OFF FOR COFFEE, JUST AS WE'D
PLANNED, AND SALIM AND THE TWO SPARK COUSINS
JOINED THE TICKET QUEUE. CHRISTY WENT OVER, PRE-
TENDING TO BE A STRANGER, ALTHOUGH HE'D MET
SALIM ONCE BEFORE. HE GAVE SALIM THE TICKET AND
SHOWED HIM HIS PLACE IN THE QUEUE AND THEN HE
DASHED OFF TO WORK BECAUSE HE WAS RUNNING LATE.

I NEARLY DIED LAUGHING PRETENDING NOT TO
KNOW SALIM. I'D TO BITE MY CHEEK ALL THE WAY TO
THE RAMP AND STILL SALIM DIDN'T LOOK AT ME, NOT

UNTIL WE WERE ON THE WHEEL ITSELF. THEN THE CAPSULE DOORS CLOSED AND WE WENT UP AND WE SPLIT OUR SIDES. IT WAS MAGIC. AIR AND LIGHT AND MILES OF LONDON, ALL TO OURSELVES. WE WERE HAPPY.

THEN WHEN WE GOT TO THE TOP SALIM WENT QUIET. HE WAS LOOKING STRAIGHT AT THE SUN.

'SALIM,' I SAID, 'WHAT'RE YOU STARING AT?'

'MANHATTAN,' HE SAID.

'IT'S LONDON,' I SAID, 'NOT MANHATTAN.'

'IT'S MY FATE, MARCUS. I'VE GOT TO FACE IT.'

I WAS SAD THEN. IT SOUNDED LIKE HE'D CHANGED HIS MIND ABOUT SWAPPING IDENTITIES, DISAPPEARING AND COMING BACK WITH ME TO MANCHESTER TO HIDE. BUT WHEN EVERYONE TURNED TO GET THE PHOTO TAKEN, HE LAUGHED AND TOOK THE WIG OFF MY HEAD AND STUCK IT ON HIS. I TOOK OFF THE JACKET HE PUT IT ON. I STRAIGHTENED THE WIG, POPPED ON THE SUNGLASSES. IT TOOK SECONDS. NOBODY SAW US. THEY WERE ALL LOOKING THE OTHER WAY FOR THEIR SOUVENIR SHOT.

THEN THE POD LANDED. WE WALKED OUT RIGHT

UNDER THE NOSES OF THE SPARK COUSINS AND YOU SHOULD HAVE SEEN THEIR FREAKED-OUT FACES. SALIM PUT ON THIS FANCY WALK, JUST LIKE A GIRL. NEXT HE CRUISED PAST WHERE HIS MUM WAS SITTING HAVING COFFEE AND SHE LOOKED STRAIGHT AT HIM AND DIDN'T RECOGNIZE HIM.

I DRAGGED HIM OFF BEFORE SHE NOTICED ME AND WE DISAPPEARED INTO THE CROWD. HE GOT HIS MOBILE PHONE OUT AND TURNED IT OFF. 'THE DAY'S OURS, MARCUS!' HE SHOUTED. HE THUMPED ME ON THE BACK AND TOOK OFF THE WIG. HE'D LEFT HIS CAMERA BEHIND WITH ONE OF THE COUSINS, BUT BETWEEN US WE STILL HAD SOME MONEY, SO HE BOUGHT A DISPOSABLE CAMERA AT A CHEMIST'S AND SNAPPED ONE OF ME ON THE BRIDGE, AND THEN HE BOUGHT HOT DOGS AND MARS BARS AND COKES AND WE PICNICKED IN THIS PARK BY THE RIVER AND I PRETENDED TO BE A DUCK SQUAWKING AND SALIM SAID I WAS A COMIC GENIUS. THEN WE WENT TO THIS SQUARE WHERE ALL THE BUSKERS PERFORM. THEY WERE DEAD FUNNY — A JUGGLER ON STILTS WITH A TEAR IN HIS PANTS, A MAGICIAN WITH A SILVER GLOBE THAT ROLLED OVER

HIS BODY, A CLOWN THAT DID TEN SOMERSAULTS AND LANDED ON HIS NOSE. AFTER THE SHOW SALIM GAVE THE CLOWN HIS LAST POUND. WE WALKED UP TOTTENHAM COURT ROAD AND FOUND THIS SHOP THAT SELLS ELECTRIC PIANOS. YOU COULD DO ORGAN, STRINGS, TRUMPETS AND DRUMBEATS ALL AT ONCE. IT WAS GREAT, THE BEST DAY I'D EVER HAD. I WANTED IT TO LAST FOR EVER. BUT IT DIDN'T.

WE GOT TO EUSTON STATION. THAT'S WHEN SALIM TOLD ME HE WASN'T COMING WITH ME.

'I CAN'T, MARCUS,' HE SAID.

'YOU CAN. IT'S EASY. YOU HOP ON AND HIDE IN THE BOG.'

'IT'S NOT THAT. I CAN'T RUN AWAY. NOT FROM MY MUM. SHE'S SOME MUM, MY MUM. BUT SHE'S THE ONLY MUM I'VE GOT. AND IT'S NOT JUST HER. IT'S THE COUSINS. TED AND KAT.'

'THE SPARKS? THOUGHT YOU SAID YOU COULDN'T CARE LESS ABOUT THEM.'

'THAT WAS BEFORE I MET THEM AGAIN. THEY'RE GREAT, KAT AND TED. IF I DON'T GO BACK, THEY'LL GET INTO TROUBLE FOR LETTING ME GO

ON THE EYE BY MYSELF. AND MUM WILL BE FRANTIC.'

I DIDN'T KNOW WHAT TO SAY. PEOPLE RUSHED BY, DASHING FOR TRAINS. ANNOUNCEMENTS DRONED ON. I HEARD ONE FOR MANCHESTER: MY TRAIN.

'YOU'RE JUST A MOSHER-WANNABE,' I SAID.

'YEAH. YOU'RE THE REAL MOSHER, MARCUS. I'M NOT IN YOUR LEAGUE.' HE SMILED. 'YOU DID THE MAGGOTS, DIDN'T YOU?'

'HOW D'YOU KNOW?'

'WHEN I WAS ROUND YOUR HOUSE LAST, YOUR DAD TOLD ME ABOUT HIS HOBBY. FISHING.'

THEN HE GAVE ME BACK SHANNON'S PINK FLUFFY JACKET AND I PUT IT IN MY BACKPACK ALONG WITH THE WIG. BUT I MADE HIM KEEP THE SUNGLASSES. THEY LOOKED GOOD ON HIM. A WHISTLE BLEW. IT WAS MY TRAIN. WE SAID GOODBYE AND HE HUGGED ME.

'RUN, MARCUS. I'LL SEND YOU A CARD FROM THE EMPIRE STATE BUILDING.'

SO I RAN. DOORS WERE SLAMMING AND I HEARD HIM SHOUT AFTER ME, 'DON'T LET THEM CALL YOU PAKI-BOY. YOU'RE MOSHER MARCUS, REMEMBER? YOU'RE A COMIC GENIUS.'

A GUARD SAW ME AND SHOUTED. I JUMPED ON THE TRAIN. I ONLY JUST MADE IT BEFORE THEY LOCKED THE DOORS. I SAW SALIM WAVING AS THE TRAIN PULLED OUT. IT WAS THE LAST TIME I SAW HIM.

I HID IN THE TOILET UNTIL AFTER STOKE-ON-TRENT. AT MANCHESTER I GOT OFF WITHOUT GETTING CAUGHT AND WENT HOME. 'HOW WAS THE SCOUTS?' MUM ASKED.

'FANTASTIC,' I SAID.

LATER THAT NIGHT, WHEN I WAS SNEAKING SHANNON'S PINK JACKET BACK INTO HER WARDROBE, I FOUND SALIM'S MOBILE PHONE IN THE POCKET. HE'D LEFT IT BEHIND, JUST LIKE HE'D LEFT HIS CAMERA WITH THE COUSINS. I'D MAIL IT TO HIM WHEN HE GOT TO NEW YORK, I THOUGHT, AND PUT IT IN MY DESK DRAWER.

THE NEXT DAY THE POLICE CAME. THEY SAID SALIM HAD GONE MISSING. MUM WAS THERE. IF I'D ADMITTED TO HAVING BEEN WITH SALIM THE DAY BEFORE, SHE'D HAVE BEEN LIVID. SO I STUCK TO THE SCOUTS STORY. BUT AFTER THE POLICE LEFT, I STARTED WORRYING. WHERE WAS SALIM? WHY HADN'T

HE GONE BACK TO THE SPARKS' HOUSE LIKE HE'D SAID?

I TOSSED AND TURNED ALL NIGHT. THEN TODAY I COULDN'T TAKE IT ANY MORE. I TOOK OUT HIS PHONE, MEANING TO CALL HIS MUM AND TELL HER WHAT I KNEW. SO I DID. I TURNED IT ON. THERE WERE ABOUT TWENTY VOICEMAIL MESSAGES WAITING, ALL FROM HER. SHE SOUNDED TERRIBLE. I PUT THROUGH A CALL BUT IT RANG AND RANG. THEN SHE ANSWERED AND I REALIZED I COULDN'T FACE TALKING TO HER. I HUNG UP AND SWITCHED THE PHONE OFF AGAIN. I HID IT UNDER MY MATTRESS.

THEN, LATER, CHRISTY RANG ME ON MY MOBILE. HE SAID SALIM'S COUSINS HAD BUMPED INTO HIM AT THIS MOTORBIKE SHOW WHERE HE'S WORKING. HE HADN'T GIVEN ME AWAY, BUT IF I KNEW WHERE SALIM WAS, I'D BETTER GO STRAIGHT TO THE POLICE AND LEAVE HIM OUT OF IT. HE SHOUTED HIS HEAD OFF.

I DIDN'T KNOW WHAT TO DO. I COULDN'T GO TO THE POLICE. I'D GET INTO TROUBLE. THEN, TONIGHT, THE POLICE SHOWED UP. AND THEY KNEW EVERYTHING. SALIM'S COUSIN TED HAD WORKED IT OUT, THEY SAID.

They said how it had been with the wig and the Eye and jumping on the train. It was like Ted Spark had been in my head, seeing my thoughts. And I remember Salim saying how he had some weird syndrome that made him think like a giant computer.

So this is the truth and nothing but the truth. I last saw Salim at Euston train station. This is all I know.

Marcus Flood

THIRTY-EIGHT

Retracing the steps

When Detective Inspector Pearce finished reading out Marcus's statement, it was 10.03 p.m.

Aunt Gloria looked at Marcus with an expression that was off the Richter scale. Her bottom lip hung down, tears fell down that she didn't bother to wipe away. Rashid sat on the dining chair completely motionless, his head between his hands. Detective Inspector Pearce leaned forward, her knuckles tight.

'Marcus,' she said, 'I want you to think. Take your time. Was there anything Salim said – anything – that might give us a clue to where he went next?'

Marcus's hood shook. 'No. That's it. I've told you everything I remember. He said he was coming straight back here. Honest to God.'

'Did he say how?'

'No. He had a travel card. He'd shown me it earlier.' He pulled the hood down more over his face.

The policewoman who was looking after him put an arm round him.

'I want to go home now,' came his voice, muffled.

Detective Inspector Pearce nodded. 'Take him home,' she said. 'If he remembers anything else, call me right away.'

Marcus was led to the door, but just as he was about to go, Aunt Gloria stood up.

'Marcus,' she said. The room went quiet. Marcus paused, but didn't turn round.

'I want you know, Marcus. Know it from me, Salim's mother. This was none of your fault.'

Then she sat down and groaned.

Marcus shuffled over to her. 'I forgot,' he said. 'To give you this.' He held out his hand. In it was Salim's mobile. Aunt Gloria took it from him with shaking fingers. She held it up to her cheek.

'Oh, Salim,' she whispered to it. 'Where are you?'

Marcus and his police escort left.

Detective Inspector Pearce touched Aunt Gloria on the shoulder and said how she was going back to headquarters to mount a London-wide search. The workers in the underground, the bus drivers who went through Euston would be questioned. She'd leave no stone unturned, she said. Then she left too and Aunt Gloria started to cry again.

Then Mum sent Kat and me up to bed.

We didn't even try to go to sleep. Kat sat up on the lilo. I sat up in my bed. I had the bedside light on. My head thumped.

'Ted?' Kat said.

'What?'

'You thought you'd found him. And you hadn't. He's gone again.'

'Yes, Kat. Gone.'

'I don't like it, Ted.' She shivered. 'Inspector Pearce doesn't like it either.'

'No.'

'All along she thought Salim had run away. Now she doesn't think so any more.'

'No.'

'There are only two possibilities, Ted.'

'What?'

'Either he ran away. Or he was kidnapped.'

'Kidnapped?'

'Yes.'

'But why? Aunt Gloria isn't a millionaire, is she?'

'Oh, Ted. You're so young. Kids get kidnapped for other reasons.'

'What other reasons?'

'Stop looking at me like a duck that's forgotten how to quack!'

I stopped tilting my head and blinked. 'What other reasons, Kat?'

'Sex stuff.'

My hand shook itself out.

Kat lay down, curling up. She didn't go to sleep. I heard no lapping like a dog drinking. After a long while I turned the radio on low. It was the shipping forecast, at midnight. '*The general synopsis at o-o-hundred hours issued by the Met Office . . . Fitzroy, mainly northerly, five or six becoming variable, thundery . . . Forth Tyne Dogger six or seven . . .*' Down south, the rain came in. The winds rose. I heard tree branches tapping the roof of our garden shed. I thought of the washing on the line, soaked again.

Squalls of hard raindrops drummed against the window. I got out my weather book and looked up the section on the Coriolis effect. I heard Salim's voice, at Euston Station, talking to Marcus. *They're great, Kat and Ted.*

I thought of the boy on the slab. I thought of Salim, somewhere in the great silent void, or lying somewhere out there in the growing storm. Two possibilities. Hiding or kidnapped.

'Switch it off, Ted. The radio. It's driving me nuts.'

It was Kat. I switched it off.

'I can't sleep,' she moaned.

'Kat, you know the theories? The nine theories?'

'Not them again, *please.*'

'One of them was right, wasn't it?'

'Yeah. Number six. Clever-clogs.'

'But you remember how I first thought of eight, and then later I thought of a ninth?'

'So?'

'Maybe what you said earlier isn't true.'

'What d'you mean?'

'You said there are only two theories. Either he's

hiding or he's kidnapped. But maybe there's a third theory. Like the ninth one before. One that we haven't yet thought of.'

Kat was listening now. She got up and switched on the main light. 'Now you're talking,' she said. 'A third theory. There must be one.'

She walked up and down beside the lilo, thumping a fist into her palm, like a stone hitting paper in the stone-scissors-paper game you play when you are small. It was the one game I knew how to play and it was my favourite. I made a scissors out of my hand. It was like the third theory we were trying to find.

I thought out loud. 'Maybe Salim went missing again deliberately. Willingly. Maybe Marcus is lying.'

Kat stopped pacing. She looked at me. 'Marcus was telling the truth.'

'How do you know?'

'I just know. It's a body-language thing, Ted. Like how I knew that the ninth theory was wrong. It's the same now. I just know it was the way Marcus said. Salim didn't mean to vanish. He meant to come back here. He'd changed his mind about running away.'

'So that means he vanished unwillingly.'

'Yeah.' She sat down on the bed. 'There are only two possibilities, Ted. There *are* only two theories. He either vanished of his own accord – or of somebody else's.'

'Somebody else's,' I repeated.

'Which means that somebody – out there – is holding him.'

'Holding him.' I got out of bed and opened the window. 'Somebody out there,' I repeated. The northeasterly wind blew in. The papers on my desk flew across the room. A leaf came in. I thought about the Coriolis effect. I could smell the outside. I could smell London.

'Somebody out there,' Kat whispered, joining me at the window. She put her arm around my shoulders.

'Or some thing,' I said.

The gale came into the room for a few seconds more, then Kat shut the window again. 'What d'you mean – *some thing*?'

'I don't know,' I said. 'Maybe something got in

Salim's way and deflected him off course. Like the Coriolis effect. That puts the wind off course all the time. And it's not a person. It's a thing. It's a thing you can't even see.'

'D'you mean – he met with an accident?'

'I don't know. Maybe.'

'OK. He met with an accident of some kind and couldn't get home. But he'd have shown up – his body would have been found. Or he'd be in a hospital somewhere. The police would have found him. Unless—' Kat's hands went up to her neck. Her eyes went large and round.

'Unless what?' I said.

'Unless he fell in the river. Unless he drowned.'

I thought of the cormorants ducking and diving. My hand flapped.

'You don't just fall in the river, Kat. There are walls all around. You'd have to throw yourself in deliberately.'

Kat gasped. Her eyes got even bigger. 'Maybe Salim did. Throw. Himself. In.'

'No,' I said.

Kat stared. I put my flapping hand on her soft, bony shoulder.

'No,' I said.

She breathed out. 'No. You're right. Salim wouldn't do that. He wouldn't.' She shook her head. 'OK. So this Coriolis thingy. What was it?'

'I don't know,' I said. I put my hands up to my head and shook it. 'I'm trying to think. But my brain's tired.'

'Let's be Salim, Ted. Let's both imagine we're on Euston Station. Let's retrace his steps. In our heads. Remember. He doesn't know London well. He has a travel card. Right?'

'Right, Kat.'

'He's waving Marcus goodbye. Got that?'

'Yes.'

'Then what?'

'He looks at his watch. It's four o'clock,' I said.

'And he knows Auntie Glo will be frantic. So he goes to get out his phone.'

'And he realizes he doesn't have it. He left it in the pink fluffy jacket.'

'So he goes to a public phone, right?' She frowned.

'Wrong. He didn't have the money, Kat. He'd spent it all. The disposable camera. The Mars bars. The Cokes. The busker.'

'Yeah – of course. All he's got is a travel card. So he decides to just get home.'

'He goes down the underground.'

'How do you know, Ted?'

'It's the fastest. And the easiest if you don't know London.'

'OK. He looks at the underground map. He's already been on the Northern Line this morning. He's not stupid. And it's simple. From Euston to our stop it's direct, no changing. Easy. He goes to the platform. He gets on.'

'Euston. Tottenham Court Road. Leicester Square. Embankment. Waterloo,' I said.

'Then on to our stop, Ted.'

'He gets out.'

'He gets the lift.'

'He's back to ground level, Kat.'

'He shows his travel card, or puts it through the

barrier, and then he's back. Back here! We're just round the corner from the tube.' Kat blew out a hot, angry breath. 'It's useless, Ted.'

'He might have got confused about which direction to take when he got out on the main road. I do.'

Kat stared at me. 'I don't think so. Not Salim. He'd walked the way with us just that morning. It's dead easy – just two hundred metres down the main road, past the Barracks, and then left onto Rivington Street. And then our house, halfway down.'

I nodded. 'Our house. Halfway down.'

Kat slumped back down on her lilo. 'It's useless, Ted.'

'Useless,' I said.

My hand started shaking itself out. My head went off to the side. 'What did you say, Kat?' I said. 'Say it again.'

'Useless.'

'Not that. What you said before. From the bit about the main road.'

'"Two hundred metres down on the main road,

past the Barracks, and then—"' She stopped. She stared.

'In the pod, Kat. At the top. Marcus said he was staring straight at the sun. He was looking south.'

'He said he was looking at Manhattan,' Kat murmured.

'He wasn't looking at Manhattan, Kat. Or the sun. He was looking at something that reminded him of Manhattan. A big tower block. He was looking at the Barracks.'

'That's the *some thing*,' Kat said. 'That's it. That's the Coriolis thingy. The thing that made him go off course.' Then she shook her head. 'But Ted – he was anxious to get home. Surely he wouldn't have stopped and gone wandering off into the Barracks?'

'He likes tall buildings, Kat,' I said.

Kat nodded. 'He had his disposable camera. He might have wanted to take some pictures.'

I nodded. 'It was a fine day, Kat. Good views.'

'Views which he knew soon wouldn't exist any more . . . Besides, Ted, he may have dreaded Auntie Glo going ballistic when he showed up. A little delay was maybe appealing . . . he goes into the Barracks, just for a quick look . . . then what?'

'Dad came home that evening,' I squeaked. 'He said he'd made it secure. He'd locked it up. He hasn't been back since. He said he'd been down Peckham today. On another site. He locked it up, Kat. With Salim inside it. And nobody's been there since. Salim's in there, Kat. Trapped. And the concrete crushers are going in. Tomorrow.'

THIRTY-NINE

Night Rain

'**M**other of God,' Kat shrieked. She ran out of the room. 'Dad! Mum! Come quickly.'

When I talk to people about something I've found out, they don't listen. When Kat does, everybody listens. Within five minutes everybody was half dressed and out of the door, into the driving rain. Dad brought two torches and his massive bunch of work keys. We ran down the road – Rashid, Aunt Gloria, Mum, Dad, Kat and I – with coats flapping, umbrellas blowing inside out, hearts pounding, hopes rising, my hand shaking itself out. Dad's hand trembled as he undid the padlock. A great howl of wind moaned its way round the big dark tower above us. Mum held a torch. We crossed a muddy strip of grass and peeled around the back of the building to the entrance. Another key. Another shaking hand. 'Hurry, hurry!' screamed Aunt Gloria, almost grabbing the keys off Dad.

We were in. The door closed behind us. Dad

played the torch around the lobby. It stank like bad toilets and dead animals. Another key to a room, set back in the darkness. It was like an engine room. Pipes, boilers, cables, fuse boxes. It was silent like a morgue. The torch picked out what Dad was looking for. A cupboard. He unlocked that with a fourth key. There was a switch. He turned it on. Then he turned on a row of switches by the door.

Light. The tower-block lobby came alive. Yet another door to the stairwell, another key, more lights.

'Salim! Salim!' we shouted.

Up and up. Floor after floor. Kat and I were the fastest. I knew where Salim would be. He'd be right at the top on the twenty-fourth storey. By floor fifteen I was rasping. Kat was half a flight ahead. I heard her moaning and whimpering, 'Salim, uh-uh-uh, Salim.'

Our lungs had given out by the time we got to the top. Kat had a stitch.

'Salim,' she said. It was little more than a whisper.

There were four doors on each floor.

The first three we tried were locked. The fourth was ajar. I felt something scuttle past my foot in the darkness.

'Salim . . .' Kat faltered. She grabbed my hand. It was clammy and cold, but it kept my hand from shaking itself out.

'Don't go in there, Ted. I don't like it. I don't like the way it smells. Let's wait. For Dad.'

We waited hand in hand on the twenty-fourth storey, by the open door, the door that led into darkness. It was the longest wait of my life. The theories, all of them, the photos, the words on the T-shirt, the pods on the Wheel were like floating strands in my brain. There were no more theories. This was the last one, the only hope.

My heart thumped. My eardrums pounded. It was the sound of time.

Dad came, panting. He had the torch. He staggered into the dark doorway. Kat and I crept after him.

'Salim?' he said. He pushed through another door. The torch beam quivered across some grimy walls.

'Salim?'

That's where we found him. He was shaking all over, just waking from sleep. He was curled up like a foetus in an empty room on an old mattress that the last people to leave the Barracks had left behind in the flat. He was alive. Aunt Gloria rushed in and hurled herself down on him.

'Salim!' she sobbed. 'Oh, Salim. My love, my love.'

FORTY

After the Storm

Voices, tears, reconciliations: I remember them as waves of words, going back and forth, running over my head, around, past, through me. I walked to the window and pinched my nose to block out the smell of a building that Dad said was sick and I had to agree. Somewhere pigeons cooed. They'd got in through a broken window. Cold air brushed my cheek.

Somebody took me by the shoulder. It was Dad. While Mum and Aunt Gloria helped Salim to his feet and wrapped him in their coats, we looked out. The gale blew itself out and a new push of air, cool and calm, stole in. The moon appeared from behind a bank of cloud.

That's when I saw it. London, from the twenty-fourth floor, lit up like frost on glass. The dome of St Paul's was a luminous curve straight ahead. To the left was the white Eye. It was motionless, a giant bicycle wheel in the sky that did not turn.

And we went home.

In a hoarse, shaky voice, Salim told us what had happened. He had starved for nearly three days. He'd found water in a toilet cistern in the flat. That is what he drank.

He'd tried to shout from the window on the twenty-fourth floor. Nobody heard. Nobody looked up.

He'd tried to get into other flats. They were all locked.

He'd tried to get out of the stairwell. The door at the bottom was bolted.

He tried to break out of the building a thousand and one ways. But he couldn't.

He was trapped. All he could do was wait and hope. He sat where there was light and a view, in the empty flat on the twenty-fourth floor. He slept on the abandoned mattress despite its dank smell. He had half a Mars bar left from his outing with Marcus, a disposable camera, the clothes he had on and nothing more.

Then our doctor came to check him over. He

pronounced him shocked but strong. He said how
brave Salim was to have endured what he had and
prescribed a bowl of soup and bed. Dad phoned the
police and told them how we'd found him.

The next day Aunt Gloria, Rashid and Salim
talked quietly together all morning in the living
room. I don't know what they said, but afterwards
Aunt Gloria announced that Salim wanted to give
New York a trial period of six months. This time it
was his wish, she said, not just hers.

Rashid left. He thanked us for what we'd done.
He said he'd never forget. He and Salim would visit
us often, he promised, when Salim came home for
the holidays. As he walked through the front door
into our postage-stamp-sized front garden, he turned
and looked at Aunt Gloria, who stood beside me.
Aunt Gloria's hand fastened itself hard on my
shoulder.

'Gloria,' he said.

'Rashid,' she said.

A moment passed. Rashid shrugged. His eyes
were like Salim's, I realized, dark lozenges. 'Enjoy the

Big Apple,' he said. The corners of his lips went up very slightly. He waved a hand.

'We'll try, Rashid,' she said. 'Goodbye.'

'Goodbye.' His hand dropped to his side. His shoulders went down. Then he turned away and walked down Rivington Street. My head went off to the side as I watched him recede and he looked back one last time before disappearing round the corner.

After Rashid left, Salim asked to see Kat and me. He was plumped up on pillows on the sofa. His faint moustache had grown back, more noticeably than before. I remembered what he'd said about grass and lawnmowers. He wanted to know everything, how we'd worked it out. He smiled at each bit of the story, especially the bit about the motorcycle show. Kat told him most of it.

When she got to the end, she said, 'Salim, I just have to face it. My weirdo brother's a genius.'

Salim looked at me. 'You're a neek all right, Ted. Only it's got nothing to do with nerds and geeks. It's short for *unique*.'

Kat and Salim laughed at that, so I did too. And

that was when I knew I had five friends now, not three – Mum, Dad, Mr Shepherd, Kat and Salim – and I was pleased.

'What was the worst thing about being trapped in that block, Salim?' Kat said.

Salim shrank back into the pillows. 'Ugh. You don't *really* want to know?'

'Yes, we do,' Kat said.

'The noises, I guess. The noises at night. I'd lie on the mattress and hear the wind. Moaning around the tower, up, down, everywhere. Then the patters and sighs started, odd gurgles. Noises I didn't understand. I couldn't place them. Scuttles – creatures scooting across walls? Rats? Cockroaches? And flaps of wings – bats or birds? I lay in the dark, I put my jacket over my head, I buried my ears under my arms, but I could still hear them. Then something landed on my cheek, just a scrape. I sat up and screamed my head off . . .'

'OK – OK,' Kat said, blocking her ears. 'Sorry I asked.'

'It wasn't *all* bad,' Salim said.

'No?'

'During the day, it was OK. I watched the weather. I was close to the clouds. There was this thunderstorm. I saw lightning flickering over London, and these dark sheets of rain moved in, and then the sun came out. I took photos. Buildings and sky. One half of London was dark, the other light and sunny. The river was in both halves, a thin, silver line, and what divided it all was the Eye, big and white. I took a photo, Kat, the last one on the disposable camera. But the best I ever took.'

That afternoon Kat and I had a final visit from Detective Inspector Pearce. Dad and Mum sat and listened while Kat told her everything that we'd thought and done. Detective Inspector Pearce's lips turned upwards at the end.

She looked at me. 'Some brain,' she said.

She looked at Kat. 'Some action,' she said. 'You two have everything it takes to make first-class police detectives.'

'Dunno,' Kat said, dubious. 'I fancy the fashion trade.'

I told her I was destined for the Met Office.

'Pity,' she sighed. 'My colleagues say I'm a good detective. You have to be, if you're a woman in the Force. But you two have taught me something. Youngsters are more worth listening to than a legion of adults. If it weren't for you two, Salim might still be trapped in that tower block. And by now the concrete crushers would have done their worst. I dread to think . . .' She shook her head. 'We looked high and low. North and south. And all along he was right round the corner.'

Then Dad said, 'I just don't understand how Salim got himself locked in like that. I had a security guard posted at the gate. And I checked each floor, one by one, to make sure it was empty.'

It was a few phone calls later before we knew what had happened. Salim said that as he'd walked past the block, he'd noticed the gate to the boarded-up fence ajar. It was a magnet. He thought of the twenty-four floors, the views that would soon no longer exist, his disposable camera. He'd be only a few minutes, he'd promised himself. He'd slipped in.

Nobody was about. He'd found the main entrance, then the door to the stairwell. He'd cruised up the stairs.

Meanwhile Dad had been checking each floor was vacated, the last tenants all gone. He'd posted his colleague Jacky Winter as a guard at the outer gate while he'd gone up, using the stairs, until he got to the top.

'You rang me, Faith, to say that Salim had gone missing, just as I was on the twenty-fourth floor, in the vacated flat. I remember rushing out – I left the door to the flat unlocked. It was no big deal, since the building would be secure from below. To save time I took the lift back down to the lobby. Just as Salim was coming up the stairs, I guess. I locked all the doors in the lobby area. I turned off the water and electricity. I went outside. I locked the main entrance. There was Jacky, by the fence gate, where I'd left him. We padlocked the gate together – and left.'

Salim swore he'd seen no sign of a guard.

Jacky Winter was questioned. At first he denied

having left his post. Then he broke down and admitted it. He'd nipped to the newsagent's. He'd only been gone two minutes. He'd been dying for a smoke and had 'run out of fags'.

He lost his job.

FORTY-ONE

The Last Turn of the Wheel

Two days later we saw Salim and Aunt Gloria off at the airport. Salim grinned at me and shook my hand hard before they went through passport control.

'Mr Unique,' he said. 'See you in New York.'

Mum and Aunt Gloria embraced in their usual embarrassing way.

Dad went to kiss Aunt Gloria on the cheek but missed and kissed the air instead.

Aunt Gloria gave Kat, then me, her hot, hard hug. Just as I squirmed away, she grabbed my wrist.

'Here, Ted,' she said. 'Take these and throw them away. I don't need them any more.' She thrust her cigarette holder and cigarette case at me and fanned her face as if she could no longer stand the thought of smoke.

Then she smiled and I remembered to smile back and that was how Aunt Gloria became my sixth friend.

'C'mon, Mum,' Salim said. 'We'll miss our flight.'
He tugged her sleeve. They waved a last goodbye.
Salim looked at me over his shoulder as the guard
checked his passport. We were eyeball to eyeball,
just as we'd been when we'd first met. He winked.
I'm not sure if I got it right, but I scrunched up one
of my eyes as hard as I could.

Their plane took off as a large Atlantic high
asserted itself across Lundy and Fastnet. It stayed fair
with moderate winds for the duration of their flight.

When we got home, Dad said he was going to
spend the weekend in bed. But he didn't. He began
cooking eggs, whistling the *Laurel and Hardy* theme
tune, as if the hurricane that was Aunt Gloria had
never been. 'I'm making my special omelette, Faith,'
he said. 'The one you used to like when we were
dating.'

Mum rolled her eyes but smiled at the same time.

'Will I like it?' Kat asked.

'If your mum does, you will,' Dad said. 'Because I
know and Ted knows too, don't we, Ted?'

'Hrumm,' I said. 'Know what?'

'Mum and Kat are like two peas in a pod. That's why they argue all the time.'

Mum looked at Kat.

Kat shrugged. 'Takes one to know one,' she said. They smiled.

After the omelette, which was very good to eat, Mum announced that Aunt Gloria and Rashid wanted Kat and me to have a present for what we'd done. Kat admitted to the fifty quid we'd not given back since being at the Eye. She gave Mum what was left over from our investigations. Mum laughed when she heard how we'd spent it. She insisted it didn't count. We could still have something else.

'What – anything?'

'Anything within reason.'

I chose a weather watch. It's an amazing invention. It tells the time, but it also has an excellent compass and different modes. When you press a button, it becomes a mini barometer, showing the air pressure. My weather predictions have increased in accuracy by 31.5 per cent.

Kat said she wanted a motor scooter.

Mum shrieked, 'Don't be ridiculous, Kat. You're too young.'

'Aw, Mum – you *said*—'

'Within reason, Kat.'

'OK, OK. Can I have my hair cut and coloured at Hair Flair, then?'

Hair Flair was where she'd gone for a consultation when she'd gone AWOL from school that day. Mum sighed. 'All right – Hair Flair it is,' she said.

Kat came home later that day with her brown hair cut into different lengths, with a long uneven fringe that kept falling over her eyes and dirty blonde streaks like rain makes when it goes down a windowpane. I wondered how she could see to walk. Mum's mouth opened but no sound came out. Dad glanced up at Kat over his newspaper and disappeared behind it again. The newsprint shuddered.

'Don't you like it?' Kat said, her voice going upwards.

My head went off to one side. 'Kat,' I said.

'*What?*'

I could have said she looked like a sheepdog that had forgotten how to bark, but I didn't. 'It's a real cool haircut, Kat.'

Through the strands of fringe, she smiled.

My third lie. I wrote it down in my new silver folder, called *My Lies*. It's in my desk drawer and it's got a lot of growing to do.

Just as planned, the Barracks got knocked down. Our neighbourhood looked odd at first, as if a giant alien presence had been beamed to another planet, leaving behind naked sky. Then I realized. Since it's gone there's a different view. When you walk down our street, just as you turn onto the main road, for an instant, you see half the Eye. You almost have to pinch yourself. It looks unreal, as in Kat's dream. It's moving so slowly you'd hardly know. The capsules of glass and steel glitter. The white spokes wobble in the sun's glare. And always, Salim's silhouette is there, hovering in the centre, waving to us just as he did that day. Salim or not Salim. Salim

Supreme. It's as if the moment he boarded, 11.32 a.m., 24 May, floats on in a time warp somewhere in my brain.

Acknowledgements

My warmest thanks are due to the following people, without whose encouragement I could not have written this story: Marie Conan, Fiona Dunbar, Oona Emerson, Geoff Morgan and my nieces Sophie Theis and Siobhan Emerson, who gave important feedback on plot intricacies. Maximum thanks also go to Hilary Delamere, who went around this particular London Eye three times over. I am greatly indebted to Sophie Nelson's sharp copy-editing eyes and, as ever, to the wondrous editorial quartet that is Annie Eaton, David Fickling, Kelly Hurst and Bella Pearson.

THE PENDERWICKS
By Jeanne Birdsall

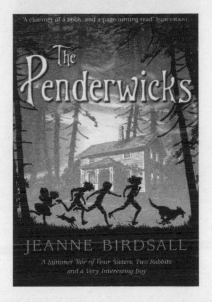

Meet the Penderwicks: Rosalind, Skye, Jane and Batty. Four
sisters, all as different as chalk and cheese. When the girls, their
father and Hound the dog head off on holiday, little do they
know they are about to enjoy a summer that will change their
lives. Instead of the cosy cottage they expect, they find themselves on a beautiful estate called Arundel. Soon the girls are
discovering the magic of the sprawling gardens and treasure-
filled attic, and they meet a boy called Jeffrey, who becomes a
friendly accomplice in all their adventures.

But the girls also gain an enemy: Mrs Tifton, the ice-hearted
owner. She gives them dire warnings to stay out of trouble –
something that proves impossible for the accident-prone
Penderwicks . . .

WINNER OF THE US NATIONAL BOOK AWARD 2005

978 0 385 61034 6

INTO THE WOODS
by Lyn Gardner

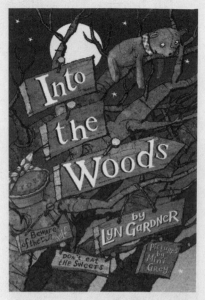

Aurora Eden's List of VERY Important
Things to do Today

1. Tell Storm off for making fireworks – AGAIN!
2. Bake chocolate-coated madeleines.
3. Dust behind the kitchen cabinets – IMPORTANT!
4. Ask Storm if she knows anything about that
funny-looking musical pipe I found behind the pickle jars.
5. See if Desdemona has laid any eggs.
6. Set Storm ESPECIALLY hard maths test as
punishment for crying WOLF.
7. Make sure no one finds out we are living without a Grown-up.
8. Convince Storm that Witches Aren't Real.
9. Rearrange linen cupboard.
10. DON'T GO INTO THE WOODS!

978 0 552 55459 6